City of the Fallen

Dark Tides series, Book One

Diana Bocco

BOOKS

CHAPTER 1

Her last night of freedom.

Isabelle looked into the distance one more time before she closed the shutters and started securing the windows. The air was thick with moisture and a storm was brewing in the distance, making the darkening sky appear even more ominous and somber than usual.

Over the past few years she had grown used to the silence, to the disappearance of cars, music, children. Still, tonight everything seemed even more dreary than usual. Maybe because she knew it was her last night of hiding out in the shadows. Her last night of holding on to what it meant to be human.

The rest of the group was busy latching the windows, but she couldn't tear herself away from the last bit of light scurrying in through the gap in the shutters. She pushed her face against the wood and took a deep breath, trying to sponge up the sunset into her lungs. The air smelled bare, just like it had for years now.

Two years ago, on her twenty-ninth birthday, she had promised herself she would die before letting one of the monsters touch her. Now, she was ready to walk into the darkness and offer herself to them.

The chances of her making it through the barren lands and into the compound were small. If she managed to get there before the sun went down and they woke up, maybe she had a chance. A small one, but a chance nonetheless.

Her body pulsated in fear and anticipation. She didn't want to think about what was waiting for her when she finally made it there. Surviving the monsters outside only to become a slave and then try the impossible.

"I wish you would reconsider."

She sighed before turning around to face her brother. Her baby brother, who had aged a decade since the invasion had begun five years ago and badly needed a shave.

She resisted the urge to hug him. "We've been over this before, Shawn. And you know as well as I do that there's no other way."

Shawn smiled softly. "We also know the chances of this working are very small."

Isabelle looked towards the living room to the few faces hushed up in the darkness. The whole group had been hiding in the house for almost six months, and were as close as family now. Or as close as a family you could get after everything that had happened.

They had been in the house longer than in any of their previous hideouts. Partly because the house was in a semi-rural area, away from main roads and well hidden behind rows of trees and outbuildings. Unless somebody was looking closely, it was relatively easy to miss. Besides, the group was getting weaker. Gas was in short supply and they were now down to two vehicles that barely ran anymore. Moving on foot was almost impossible. With impromptu shelters so hard to find, they couldn't risk getting caught on the roads when the sun went down.

When the invasion started, most people had run away with their families, hidden and tried to survive as best they could in the midst of the chaos that ensued. Slowly, however, most families had started to lose members. Children had been the first to go—too slow and too loud to avoid the monsters hunting in the dark. Then went the weak and the old. Without access to hospitals and medical care, it didn't take much to knock you down. And once you were down, you were easy prey. To survive, the only choice was to run and hide, so the weak ones were left behind to be hunted down like animals.

There had been no warning, no sign of the coming apocalypse. The attackers had risen out of the darkness in a matter of days. How long they'd been around, planning an invasion, was anybody's guess. But when they had decided to make their presence known, they had been ready for war. The world hadn't been. The world population had quickly died by the hundreds of millions. The ones who survived, the people like her, had been hiding in holes and blacked-out houses for five years. And it was time for a survivor to come out and play hero—even if it was a stupid idea.

She put her caramel hair up in a ponytail, thinking it had never been this long before. "We're starving, Shawn. Half of the people here are sick and we've run out of places to scavenge. What else can we do?"

He cursed and then plopped down on a chair near the window. "I'll take the first shift."

She had given up on shifts a long time ago. If the monsters found the house and decided to attack, there was nothing her group could do. Shawn probably knew that too, but he insisted on organizing watch shifts throughout the night. She didn't want to argue. This was her brother's shot at holding on to hope and she didn't want to take that away.

But deep down she knew an attack would be quick, merciless and fatal.

The monsters would win. The vampires.

~*~

The first sliver of sun was peeking in through the windows when she woke up, breathing hard. She'd been dreaming all night about the monsters and the horrors that awaited her. The screams still resonated in her ears, almost as real as the world around her.

She sat up on her mattress and took a few deep breaths, fighting against the wild booming in her chest. As her breathing started to calm down, she looked around, pausing on the mattress where Anna and Sofia were sound asleep, just a few feet away from her. At nineteen and twenty-one, the sisters were the youngest people she had seen in a very long time.

It all suddenly seemed hopeless. Even if she was able to get to the compound, what exactly was she hoping to accomplish? Was she really expecting to walk into the king's room and stake him in the heart while the other vampires watched?

Isabelle, the great vampire killer.

She felt like crying.

Right then and there, she decided she had to leave right now, without saying goodbye. The practical side of her was telling her it was best not to waste any daylight with hugs, tears and promises of "I'll see you soon". But the truth was more complicated than that. She simply didn't want to lie. She didn't want to promise Shawn that she'd see him soon. She didn't want to deal with everybody's last-minute requests for her to stay behind. She had decided a long time ago that humanity's last hope was in killing the vampire king. And that she should be the one to try it.

It had been a fantasy at first. The kind of daydream you had when all hope was lost and you wanted to convince yourself you could still win. So she had dreamed, first during the day and then eventually every time she closed her eyes. Dreams of a new dawn, of a hopeful tomorrow. And of herself piercing the heart of the monster that ruled the vampire world. Somehow in the midst of all the dreams, she had convinced herself it was actually possible. And the dreams had become more of a strategic plan: how to get to him, how to gain his trust, how to kill him. As much as she hated the idea, the only way in was to become the one thing she hated more than vampires themselves: a pet.

The first couple of years had been easy for vampires. A plentiful supply of blood and a prey that was easy to hunt. But over time, more and more people had gone into hiding and soon vampires were having a difficult time finding food. So were humans. And so the concept of pets had been born. Those who were starving had the option of becoming pets. Either for a single vampire or—much worse—for a group of them. In exchange for providing blood, sex and entertainment, the person could get food and shelter. No more running, no more hiding.

Complete families had started surrendering in a desperate attempt to stay alive. It was hard to guess what had happened to them once they were gone from the cities and into the vampire compounds or areas. None were ever seen again. There were lots of rumors—vampires torturing children, vampires leaving humans to die once their blood supply became too low, women being passed around to a large group of vampires… It was hard to know what was true and what was a result of widespread panic. She knew vampires could turn humans if they wanted, but she doubted they ever did. Why bring a lowly human into their ranks? There were already enough of them (and too few humans) in the world.

She closed her eyes, took a deep breath to hold back the tears and then slowly got up. Robert was on window watch, the last of the day. Once the sun was up, the world was safe again—at least until the darkness returned.

He acknowledged her with a slight head nod when she entered the room.

"I'm going out for a bit," she whispered and Robert nodded again.

On the way out, she grabbed her scavenging bag. It contained everything she needed—everything she owned—plus a change of clothes she'd stolen from Sofia. She needed to clean up before walking into the compound. The more attractive she looked, the better her chances of landing an important master. Somebody closer to the king.

She jumped into the car and started the engine on the first try. Before anybody had time to step outside, and before she had a chance to change her mind, she took off towards the highway and the plundered world ahead.

The wind was howling against her window as she drove away.

Chapter 2

By five in the afternoon, the realization was sinking in: she had underestimated the distance to the compound.

Even driving at high speeds on an empty road, there would be no way she could make it there before sunset. But the roads weren't exactly deserted anyway: skeletons of abandoned cars littered the highway. At times, she had to veer off the pavement to maneuver around them. They were a reminder of how fast and how devastating the invasion had been. Many had died right there, on the highway, as the vampires descended upon them with annihilating fury.

Her major concern was to make sure she didn't get caught driving at night. The monsters would be out, hunting, and she would be the center of attention. Even worse: they would be able to hear her coming for miles. There were few cars left on the roads, in part because many had become undrivable, full of the remnants of civilization. But there was also the noise factor.

Vampires could detect the quietest of cracks miles away, so an engine would act like a magnet, bringing them out of hiding and straight towards her. She'd heard they patrolled the roads for clues of survivors. And they were growing hungrier by the day—if one of them found her, she would become dinner right then and there.

Her best chance of making it through the night was to find a hiding place and then set off again at sunrise. She could try to make it to the next town over—how far was it? Fifty miles? Seventy?—but towns didn't usually make for the best hiding places. They were too obvious. Survivors often headed there to scavenge for food, medicine or anything useful they could find.

That would've been fine, except that where humans lurked, so did vampires. The scent of blood was strong and it attracted solitary hunters. Too much of a risk. It was actually a better idea to hide somewhere barren, where humans wouldn't normally be found because there was nothing there for them. Factories were a good choice. So were airports and schools. No planes anywhere in sight, but the paper factory was close enough that she could make it there before darkness took over.

Maybe.

~*~

The factory had only been abandoned a few years, but the state of decay made it seem like it had been left to rot for decades. Even from far away, she could see most of the windows had been smashed and mold had begun to seep over the walls, blackening them. Nature had no mercy for anything or anybody, reclaiming what it could as fast as possible. Just like vampires. Just like the survivors.

Ironically, much of the destruction—if not all—you could find in the cities had been caused by humans. Vampires had no use for food, medicine or other material things found in cities. When the invasion began, most of them had simply taken over the mansions and luxurious countryside residences. As people fled from the cities trying to find somewhere to hide, even the most sprawling metropolises had become ghost towns. The vampires had no interest in them, and people couldn't stay in them without risking being discovered, so nature took over.

Before people had taken off, there had been a lot of looting, destruction, chaos. People still hadn't really grasped what was going on, so they clung to the notion of material richness. Grab nice clothes, take the expensive car with you. Soon the cities had been pillaged until they looked like warzones. Fires had broken out, people had killed each other. All without the help of vampires.

She stopped the car between two sheds and looked around. Part of the factory's roof had collapsed and flaking speckles of paint danced around in the wind and away from the walls. Moss peeked through some of the windows and looped around the broken glass. Just beyond the factory, a couple of abandoned cars and a yellow bulldozer looked almost ready to spring to life. There was enough debris around that the car looked like it belonged there. She could see a metal staircase far ahead, providing entrance to the building. She grabbed her bag and made a dash for it.

The sun was setting down behind her, giving way to the sounds of the night. Soon, all the night hunters would come out to play.

The wind whistled and howled all around her, dragging bits of leaves and dust. She shivered and zipped up her jacket as she ran up the steps. Ivy looped around the stair rail, poking her hands when she tried to hold on to gain speed.

The door was unlocked. She stepped inside and pushed the door closed behind her. Too bad there was no way of locking it. Not that it would've stopped a determined vampire, but it might have been enough to convince him the place was empty.

She was in some sort of control room. A few empty lockers and the remnants of what looked like machines littered nearly every corner. Pieces of glass blanketed the floor and her first thought was that at least she would hear the crunch if somebody made their way into the room during the night.

The stale smell of mold permeated the room, extending towards the corridors ahead. She could hear the splatter of water in the distance, but other than that, the place was quiet. No animals scurrying by—at least not yet. She needed to find a place to hide until dawn. Somewhere not only hard to reach but also where her smell wouldn't be so obvious. Both the two-legged and the four-legged predators had excellent noses. She didn't want to be found but if she was, she didn't want to be surprised in a corner, with nowhere to run.

She left the control room and hurried down a corridor on the other side of the room. There were bits and pieces of metal all over the ground and she told herself this was another place to avoid in the dark—it would be impossible to walk around silently when the floor was a minefield of rubbish. Just a careless step somewhere and the sound of her feet kicking metal would reverberate all around the place.

Darkness was quickly slipping into the building and her heart sped up. The next room would have to do, whatever it was. She couldn't risk running through the building anymore once night set in. She turned a corner and pushed a door open. The room smelled like decay, like the rest of the building. There was a tiny window on the back wall, just big enough for her to slip through. A massive desk was pushed against a corner and she decided that was it. She climbed over the top and sat on the floor, against the wall. The back of the desk was made of solid wood that touched the floor, so she wasn't visible from the other side. She glanced up towards the tiny window, trying to figure out how many seconds it would take to jump up and out through it.

She took a knife from her bag and leaned her chin on her bent knees, waiting for the night to swallow her whole.

At some point during the night, she fell into a jagged sleep. She dreamt of somber passages and predators snooping through the darkness, so close to her that she could almost feel their breath on her skin.

She woke up gasping for air in a pitch-black room. For a second, she couldn't figure out where she was and every muscle in her body screamed for her to get up and run. She extended her hand and touched the cold wood in front of her and suddenly remembered her safe corner in the factory.

Then she heard it.

The first crack had been barely noticeable and easy to blame on the many night critters living in the factory. The next one was a lot harder to ignore. Her senses clicked into high alert, so when she heard the rustling sound of fabric shifting, she knew she wasn't alone. Part of her wanted to jump out in case the visitors were human, but her mind knew better. She forced her ears to adjust to the silence. None of the agitated breathing of the fugitive, no careless knocking against walls or accidentally kicking some rubbish on the ground. No, whoever—whatever—was walking around could see in the dark.

She had decided long ago that there was an elegance to the silence that surrounded vampires. They walked without disturbing the air around them, except for the occasional thump or crack of things shifting as they moved.

The thick darkness enveloped everything. How far was sunrise? Despite her efforts to stay perfectly still, her body was trembling, her ears pulsing. The drumming in her chest was so loud she wondered if they could hear it, smell the blood rushing through her veins.

Crack. Crack.

Two of them. Maybe more. The sounds were so inconsistent and so subtle, it would've been easy to pretend they weren't there.

The elegance of monsters, her mind screamed. It was a clever trick, one that many would fall for in a desperate attempt to hold on to sanity. Hold on to the hope that death wasn't coming.

Crack. Crack. Crack.

The sounds were getting closer, which meant they were moving down the corridor—probably inspecting every room as they went along. She had to make a decision and make it quickly. She could stay where she was, frozen, and hope they gave up before they reached her room. Or she could get up and try to scurry away to another section of the factory. Both options were equally terrifying.

She closed her eyes and tried to steady her heart. Pictures of her body being drained of blood flashed in her mind. *Get out, Isabelle,* she told herself. *You have to get out* now.

She focused on the sounds for what felt like an eternity. Moonlight was streaming through the small window and she tried to guess how far sunrise was. A couple of hours? Minutes away? She considered jumping out of the window, but that would mean breaking the glass first. If she did, would she have time to jump out of it before they got to her?

Crack.

The sound reverberated down the corridor. At least a hundred feet away, she guessed. Then prayed her guess was right.

Holding her breath, she slowly stood up. The room was empty. Moonlight streamed through the windows beyond the door, bathing the corridor with a phantom-like shine.

She looked at her feet, trying to discern the objects on the floor so she could avoid them. The smallest sound, just a single wrong move —and they would be on her in a second.

Before she scurried into the corridor, she paused long enough to take a deep breath. Her mind was screaming for her to turn around and go back to the false security of the desk, but she shushed the thoughts away. Instead, she stepped into the moonlight, her heart in a frenzy.

The corridor was empty too. She moved away from the moonlight melting into the building and saw the break of light painting itself on the horizon. Sunrise was just minutes away. Whatever vampires were in the building were there to hide from the coming daylight—not because they'd seen her car and were looking for her. They had probably been caught out and had to walk into whatever dark place they could find to wait for the next night.

A hint of hope sprang up but she pushed it down immediately. *Not yet,* she told herself. *Not yet.*

She took a tentative step, then another. The corridor around the corner was also empty. Although she couldn't see it clearly, she knew the door to the control room was at the other end of the corridor. If she could make it out of the factory and into her car, she could take off. They wouldn't risk following her out into the open with dawn so close.

Crack.

Her feet froze to the ground. The sound was closer than before. Too close. Did she have time to tiptoe all the way to the door? In a split second, she decided she didn't—and instead she took off running.

Crack. Crack. Crack. Whatever was there was now aware of the human running down the corridor. She didn't turn around to see if they were behind her. Or how close they were. She just kept running. The door into the control room was open. She rushed through it and darkness swallowed her. There were no windows there, no light, and her mind struggled to remember where the exit door was.

"A night of surprises, I must say."

Her whole body froze, her breath caught in her throat. The queasy feeling in her stomach got stronger and she had to force herself not to throw up.

The door. Where was the door?

"You're going the wrong way," the vampire said, a hint of a smile in his voice.

It was impossible to tell if he was lying to confuse her or just enjoying the situation.

She took a deep breath and turned around to face him. He was blocking the other entrance, the moonshine enveloping his massive body from behind and casting his face into complete darkness. The darkness was good, in a way, because she couldn't see his eyes. And that meant he couldn't charm her into submission. Or at least she hoped he couldn't.

"I'll just go," she said, even though it sounded so ridiculous.

The vampire laughed and her stomach quivered in response.

"Please, don't," he said. Then his voice got deeper, close to a roar. "You smell delicious."

She reached behind her back, looking for something solid. Nothing. She walked a step backwards into the empty space.

He didn't move and she knew he was playing with her. The way a cat played with a mouse it was about to kill. Just to enjoy the hunt longer, just to get the bite in when least expected.

"Come out and play," he said, echoing her thoughts.

Her hand found the deadbolt—and he jumped towards her. She ducked, screaming, and fell against the door. It slammed open with a loud thump. The first hints of sunlight burned into her eyes and spilled into the room. She scrambled to her feet and then ran towards the car.

As she jumped in, she dared look back and found his eyes boring into hers from the safety of the darkness. It took several minutes of speeding down the highway before her heart stopped booming against her chest in a maddening race.

~*~

It took every last ounce of daylight to make it to the compound.

At some point during the drive, she stopped at an abandoned gas station. She filled her tank with the little gas she had left in a gas can, then walked into the bathroom to change into clean clothes. The woman looking back at her from the mirror was one she barely remembered: bright bluish eyes, soft caramel hair, pretty. At least that was what she used to be called before she became a fugitive, always covered in dust.

Five years ago, she had been a medical student completing her internship, complaining to whoever would listen about the long shifts and the sleepless nights. Five years later, she would give anything to be back in the tiring corridors of a hospital. Only because at the end of the day, she would get to go home and sleep in her own bed, by her own rules.

She looked at the reflection again. She didn't have any makeup or perfume, but at least she was dirt-free. The jeans and T-shirt she'd chosen embraced every curve—and she was hoping that'd be enough to catch the eye of somebody important within the compound. The closer she got to the king, the easier her impossible mission would be. Or at least she'd have a chance that way.

She got back into the car and sped up. Darkness would be coming back soon enough and there was no way she wanted to get caught out on the roads again.

The vampires had established special "surrender points" throughout the state, where humans could walk in and offer themselves as pets. However, surrendering at any of those points would mean getting stuck there. If she wanted a chance to cross paths with the king, she needed to make it to the compound, where he lived. She'd never seen the compound before, but she had an idea of what to expect. She knew the king had taken over an old mansion and then built other structures around it. Some people said dozens, others claimed hundreds, of buildings now surrounded the main home.

There'd been human scouts before, stories passed down and spread around the country about how the vampires had built an impenetrable wall to seal the compound. She always wondered if the wall was meant to keep prisoners in or to keep something else out. Maybe they were selective about who was allowed inside the compound. Of course that meant that getting out of the compound would be impossible—if she even made it in at all. And whether she managed to kill the king or not, chances were high that she would die within those walls.

Her only hope was that her actions would create enough chaos that the whole reign would fall. Or at least falter enough for somebody else to come along and finish what she'd started.

In the distance, the outline of a wall extended into the countryside. The place was definitively a fortress. The closer she got to the structure, the faster her heart beat—and the more her stomach quivered. Her mind kept replaying the events of the night before and the effect the vampire's presence had had on her body. She knew vampires had the ability to charm their victims—cloud their minds to make them docile and responsive—and all she could think about at the moment was that she hoped they did that before touching her.

The compound looked serene, even from a distance. She couldn't see any movement and wondered whether the place was guarded at all during the daytime. The only way they could do that was to use humans as sentinels. The walls were empty of any sign of life. No watching towers either. Were they really this careless? Or was it simply a matter of confidence, knowing that the humans were no threat at all anymore—so there was no need to create any protection against them?

The feeling that washed over her was a mix of sadness and hope. Sadness that in the five years since the invasion, no human had come up with a plan to attack the place. And hope that maybe, just maybe, the vampires' lack of concern would be their demise.

The sun would be down in less than thirty minutes. She stopped the car near the compound gate—a massive metal structure that was at least fifteen feet tall—and closed her eyes. Part of her wanted to jump out and walk around, but the property was huge and she didn't want to get caught out in the open when darkness finally came.

Eyes still closed, she tried to tune in to any sound coming from inside the compound. Nothing. The silence was a lot more unnerving than she had expected.

Back in the house, they would be closing all shutters by now, sealing themselves in for the night. She thought about Shawn, her last connection to the world she knew and loved.

A light flickered on above the gate and her chest contracted. Then another light. And another. The compound was awakening.

CHAPTER 3

She stood in front of the gate for what seemed like hours, trying to figure out how to get in. The idea of knocking—or ringing some sort of doorbell—seemed ridiculous, but how else was she supposed to let them know she was there? As she extended her arms forward to touch the gate, looking for some sort of doorknob or bell, she realized they were shaking. Trying to get her heart to slow down was a lost battle, so she tried breathing in as best she could while her hands explored the cold metal.

And then the gates moved.

She jumped backwards when the clank of the gate's mechanism sprang alive. Her whole body was pulling for her to run in the opposite direction and it took every ounce of strength to keep her feet planted on the ground. The gates slid open in slow motion, revealing the inside of the compound inch by inch. She could see flashes of walls, buildings and pathways here and there—but no vampires, nobody to welcome her or pull her inside. It was like being frozen in time, waiting for destiny to come rushing forward to meet her.

The gates stopped before they reached the halfway point. The opening was big enough for her to walk right in, but not to drive her car inside. The bag hanging on her shoulder felt suddenly heavy and irksome. She took a step in. Then another. Dozens of bright lights shone in her direction—obviously meant to blind her so she couldn't see beyond a few inches in front of her eyes.

As soon as she was inside, the gates closed behind her and the lights died off. Blinded by the brightness and trying not to panic, she just stood there. Electricity had become a thing of the past for humans. The grid had gone down just months after the invasion and the entire country had been plunged into darkness since then. Besides, even if electricity was still running, turning lights on at night would've been a very bad idea. Almost like turning on a giant billboard screaming "Humans here, come get us." The shock of the flashing lights was more than just a shock to her eyes, it was a shock to the mind too, a clear sign that she had entered a new world.

When the first vampire stepped into her line of vision, all she could see was an outline of darkness and light. It seemed fitting, being blinded into submission.

And then when the vampire finally ordered her to follow him, it all became very real.

She was in.

‿*‿

By the time her vision got used to the brightness, she was inside a large room. It looked like a ballroom, with its high painted dome and colossal marble floors. Although chandeliers

19

hung from the ceiling, the lights were off and the entire room was illuminated by what seemed like a million candles. It was a smart choice, she thought, because it gave the place a slightly supernatural feel, an air of mystery that washed over her the second she stepped in. *Fit for a king,* her mind whispered. And a far cry from the destruction claiming the cities everywhere.

The vampires looking at her reminded her of the one back in the factory—the half smiles on their faces, the look of hunger painted on their features. Except these ones knew she had nowhere to run.

"Wait here."

A wave of nausea hit her. Part of her reeled with anticipation and fear, and part of her was just angry at herself for being there, for the way the world had turned out. *No turning back now, Isabelle,* her mind taunted her.

She was still trying to steady her breathing when he entered the room. She gasped and any hope of keeping her heart steady was immediately lost. There was absolutely no doubt that she was looking at the king.

He was massive. Tall, broad, powerful. Incredibly beautiful. She could guess the muscles flexing and tightening under the shirt he was wearing. A few strands of his black hair fell over his face, partially covering his eyes. Frosted silver eyes seemed to melt into a liquid dance the second they found hers.

He was... majestic. The soft movements, the silent steps that made it seem like he was gliding above the ground, the stately look in his eyes. His movements had the elegant majesty of an aristocrat, the kind a monster should not have. The trembling of fear that had been rushing through her body for the past couple of hours was gone in an instant—and a very different emotion stirred inside her.

His eyes locked on hers, almost passionate. She knew it wasn't possible. He was a monster, the reason humanity was gone, their king. *He's nothing but a killer*, she told herself. Her mind searched for more words to describe the beast standing in front of her, but she was drawing a blank because all of a sudden, all she could think about was the shadowy softness of his movements, sensual and strong and… delicious.

The air in the room felt thick and she was having trouble breathing. She closed her eyes for a second, just to regain her composure, and when she opened them again, he was right in front of her. He was fast. Inhumanly fast.

She staggered backwards in surprise, stumbling. He moved so fast, she couldn't even see his hand shooting forward to grab her—but when his fingers made contact with her skin, fire flashed through her body. The silver in his eyes danced, as if caressing her. Was he trying to charm her? Her body felt warm, aware. So very awake. None of the fog she expected to feel if he was trying to charm her, to take control over her senses.

He raised an eyebrow and let her arm go. Her skin was burning where his fingers had been.

He pointed towards a massive glass window taking over the western wall. "If I asked you to jump from that window right now, would you?"

The question was so unexpected, she had to think for a second. "What? No, of course no."

He turned away and gazed out that same window for a second. Then he fell into a chair a few steps away from her. Or maybe fell wasn't the right word. He glided in slow motion into the chair, easing down into it as if the air was sustaining him.

"What's your name?"

It made no sense to lie. "Isabelle Bryant."

Everybody she knew had given up on last names a long time ago. They no longer meant anything, except a reminder that the conventions of society no longer applied. Which was why she insisted on holding on to hers, so she wouldn't forget what it meant to be human.

"Why are you here, Isabelle?"

There was a slight accent in his voice. British? Old European English, for sure. His eyes were boring into hers, and she wondered how much he could guess just by looking at her. "For the same reason everybody is. I'm tired of struggling."

His eyes moved over her curves, heat searing in every corner and every angle he reached. *Stop it*, her mind screamed, and a second later she realized she was talking to herself rather than to him.

"You're hardly starving," he stated and there was a suggestion to his tone that made her blush.

She felt open and exposed, just standing there in front of him. It was a brilliant strategy, actually. He was sitting there like a king would—and should—observing ordinary people parading in front of him. It not only made his position of power clear, it also served as an incentive to speak. Because she was sure that nobody would be able to stand the look in his eyes for more than just a few minutes, even if he decided not to charm them.

People would talk just to get away from those eyes.

"I'm tired of running."

"Miles."

The mention of a name confused her until she realized he'd called somebody. It had been just a whisper, but somebody appeared in the room. The newcomer looked like a guard, his military-like demeanor obvious in the stoic steps and his stone face. He looked at her briefly as the king spoke to him in a whisper.

Then the king's eyes turned to her and for a second she saw something there that took her breath away.

A hint of humanity.

Fear rushed through her body the instant she saw the light in his eyes. She couldn't allow herself to think of any of them as anything other than monsters. The whole point of being here was to destroy them—and any hint of doubt, any second-guessing, would mean disaster.

In the couple of seconds her eyes moved away towards the guard, the king rushed over to where she was. Moved so fast, in fact, that she never saw him leave the chair and make his way to her.

The heat of his proximity made her body tighten. Nothing she had heard about being charmed had warned her about that. She had been expecting fogginess, something akin to being half-asleep, but all she could feel was her own body, pulsing in response to the immediacy.

He was just inches away.

"I can smell your blood from here," he whispered, and reality tied up her stomach in two.

Her feet were frozen to the ground, her heart hammering so hard she knew he could hear it. He leaned forward, inching closer to her neck. *This is it*, she told herself. But there were no teeth, no pain. Instead, he took a deep breath before moving back and into her eyes.

And then he kissed her. The surprise lasted less than a second before desire exploded like a ravaging fire through her body. Hunger so desperate she felt like she was falling. His tongue pushed against her lips, demanding entrance. With a moan, she opened her lips and let him in. He groaned into her mouth and deepened the kiss, his tongue dancing with hers, probing, exploring. There was something different about him, something almost animal. A rough, intense taste of fire flowing from his body into hers.

Something brushed against her lower lip and she realized his teeth were grazing her mouth. Firm enough that she could

23

feel them, but without breaking the skin. Rather than scaring her, the realization of what he was doing sent her heart into a frenzy. She moaned and pushed against his body, melting into his mouth. Every inch of him was hard, pulsing, more alive than any man she had ever touched.

Heat bolted down her body, coiling in her stomach before making her way down to her legs.

Without warning, he broke the kiss. A soft moan escaped her throat and it took her a second or two to get her eyes into focus again. The room was spinning and so was her head, filled with some sort of intoxicating, pulsing sound she couldn't describe. She was panting, her body shivering from the contact. Her eyes looked for his and she saw the fire exploding in them. His chest was rising up and down as rapidly as hers and suddenly it clicked. Everything she was feeling was very real. No charming, no mind tricks. Just pure raw desire.

"Why...?"

Before she could finish the question, he turned around and left the room.

When she finally got a chance to breathe again, she realized she didn't even know his name.

CHAPTER 4

Marcus sat back in his leather chair and took a deep breath. His body was still reeling with the emotions she had stirred in him.

He hadn't been looking for a pet, but there was no way he was going to let anybody else have her. In the few centuries he had been taking pets, none of them had ever been immune to charming. To say he was intrigued was an understatement.

Even before he touched her, he had felt her heart racing. Smelled her blood rushing in anticipation. For a second he had thought it was fear, and then realized it was excitement. His whole body had hardened as soon as he kissed her and felt her respond. It had made his hunger almost unbearable, to the point where he had to leave the room to avoid feeding on her right there. No, he wanted her on his bed first. He wanted to be inside her when he tasted her. The idea of a fully awake, willing human under him was something impossible to resist.

In most cases, humans were just a necessary complication. They provided food and entertainment but little else. Partly because their fear would take over as soon as a vampire touched them and the only way to calm them down enough to enjoy them was to charm them. Charming them made them docile but it also made their emotions less real. Having an awake and very willing woman in his hands was a completely different sensation. And having one who wanted him and wasn't afraid of him was intoxicating. He stirred as he imagined her body under his, pulsating and soft as he slid into her.

The distraction would be good for him. The last three months had been more challenging than he had expected. Nobody in the compound was hungry, but the supply of blood had been dwindling in other areas of the country. So much, in fact, that many vampires had taken to patrolling the roads, hoping to hunt down whatever humans they could find. He wouldn't normally care about that, except that his brother Patrick had taken the opportunity to recruit rogue vampires. To form an army that Patrick could one day use to overthrow him.

And Marcus suspected the army was getting bigger. It was impossible to compete with Patrick and his lies and false promises. He knew his brother well enough to understand that Patrick was probably promising other vampires unlimited amounts of blood—something he couldn't deliver. He'd seen Patrick in action: ruthless, quick, out to take as much blood as he could before the kill. It wouldn't take long before Patrick had exterminated the human race.

Marcus didn't particularly care much about humans, but Patrick had an even lower opinion of the human race. To his brother, humans were little more than cattle and didn't need to be treated any better. In fact, Patrick had long nurtured the idea of breeding humans. Marcus suspected that was one of the reasons he wanted to take over the throne: to start a breeding program, farming as many humans as he could and then using the females for reproduction.

Long-term planning, Patrick called it.

Marcus didn't think it was the smartest way to fix the blood problem. He had other ideas. Part of him felt responsible for the chaos of the last few years. When the invasion began, he had expected everybody to hunt responsibly—in the open, but responsibly. That was not what had happened. Centuries of hiding in the darkness had made his kind bitter and ready to strike back. As a result, many had gone out on hunting sprees, killing dozens of humans in a single night, wasting blood and lives.

By the time he had realized what was happening, it was too late. Humanity had dwindled by the millions in just months. It had never been his intention to kill off the human race. Not only because he needed human blood to survive, but also because he was sure they could find a way to coexist—a master/peasant situation that could benefit both sides.

Right now, his greatest concern was getting the rogue vampires under control. If he didn't manage to do it within the next year or so, they would destroy everything. In the meantime, though, humans were still surrendering themselves into the compound—and his kind had enough blood to last for some time.

His thoughts returned to Isabelle and her pulsing heart. The sound of her blood rushing in excitement had been hypnotic. He could almost smell her right now—and his whole body tensed at the memory.

By now, Miles would've told everybody that she belonged to the king and wasn't to be touched. Too bad the council was meeting that night and he would have to postpone a night of pleasure. He couldn't wait to see what she tasted like.

CHAPTER 5

Isabelle's mind was spinning—and not for the right reasons.

Things were going much better than she expected. Not only was she in the compound, but it seemed the king had chosen her as his personal pet. There was no doubt in her mind that the room she'd been given was a special one. The four-poster bed reminded her of the ones you would have found in fine hotels, back when hotels were anything more than abandoned buildings left to rot. There were curtains and rugs in the room, luxuries she had not seen for years. And when she extended a hand to actually touch the bed, the silkiness of the blankets felt alien.

The metal door on the back wall of the room was locked, but she guessed it connected her room to the king's. To get here, Miles had taken her to the back of the compound, through a private courtyard. This section of the compound was home to the most luxurious building and corridors and she had no doubt the king's private quarters were located there as well.

She sat down on the luscious bed and took a shaky breath. The idea of having him just on the other side of the door seemed surreal. Things had been so clear two days ago and now her body and her mind had come to an almost complete disconnect. Not that she had forgotten what she needed to do or why she was there. But it would have been a lot easier if she had found the king to be repulsive rather than incredibly alluring.

A wave of heat stirred in her stomach at the thought of him. Cursing under her breath, she stood up and walked away from the bed.

Miles had gone through her bag and taken anything that could've been considered a weapon, including a pocket knife. Then he had searched her body for anything hidden in pockets or under clothing. She had been thinking about hiding the knife in a pocket and now she was glad she hadn't. The vampire had been quick and cold in the search, touching her as little as necessary to make sure nothing went unnoticed. But she hadn't been able to help shivering at his hands on her curves. And now she couldn't stop thinking about how different they had felt to the vampire hands that had touched her just minutes before.

She looked around the room, searching for something that could be considered dangerous. Everything around her seemed to have round edges, soft corners meant to avoid piercing and damaging vampire flesh.

Clever, she thought.

She had expected to feel more like a prisoner, but the entrance door to her bedroom was unlocked. She had tried it as soon as Miles had stepped away, expecting to find it locked. When she pulled on it and the door opened, she'd actually stumbled backwards. Her heart had gone into a frenzied race as she took a step into the almost deserted courtyard. Then she had seen the vampires stealing glances her way and she decided to step back inside. In fact, for a few seconds she had wished the door had a latching mechanism so she could lock herself in.

She would wait until the morning to explore, when the vampires were sleeping.

The moon was shining in through the open drapes, bathing everything in a ghostly light. She turned on the lamp on the table next to the bed and then walked towards the wardrobe in the other end of the room. It was full of beautiful things: dresses, pants, blouses. Everything practical enough for everyday wear but still delicate and exquisite. She reached for a blouse. The soft silk slid through her fingers and her mind clicked back to the house and the people there.

A pang of guilt hit her as she took in the luxury around her —and she had to remind herself of the high price tag attached to everything. Still, it didn't make her feel much better. Maybe because she had enjoyed the kiss and that seemed like a betrayal.

A betrayal of herself, but also of the people back in the house. A betrayal of humanity.

She closed the closet door and only then saw the dark opening into another room. A bathroom—without a door. She hadn't seen running water in years, so opening the tap and seeing the clear liquid flow out felt like heaven. The long bathtub was too tempting not to try, especially with the many bottles of what she imagined were shampoo and bath gels sitting nearby.

She took a quick look towards the front door, trying to decide if she really wanted to get naked in a room with no lock. With a deep breath, she undressed quickly, afraid she'd change her mind. She sat in the bathtub before even opening the tab so she could feel every drop of water sliding over her.

She had decided before getting to the compound that she would act like the perfect pet. She'd be quiet, submissive, obedient. She would do whatever she was told to do to convince the vampires that she wasn't there to create trouble. Part of her had expected that to be a lot harder than it seemed to be so far. Since nobody had seen the inside of the compound before, all the rumors going around were just that—rumors. And like everybody else, she had expected to find something completely different than the place she was in right now.

She had expected dungeons, crowded cells with filthy humans living in deplorable conditions. She certainly hadn't expected a private bedroom and a bathtub waiting for her.

She grabbed the liquid soap and took a deep breath. A fragrance of flowery fields and open skies assaulted her senses. Clean smells were a rarity in her new world. She poured the soap on a sponge and then on her skin.

And it was then she realized she hadn't seen a single human being since stepping into the compound.

~*~

Concentrating on the meeting was proving harder than Marcus had expected. Every few minutes, his mind would drift away and focus on Isabelle. He wasn't just curious; he was also on edge. His hunger was rising, roaring inside him. It had been a long time since he'd felt so unsatisfied, so eager to feed that it was almost painful. His body was aching to taste her, to feel her under him.

It just wasn't going to happen that night.

The night before, there had been an attack on the compound. Or, rather, an attempt at infiltration. His guards

31

had caught a rogue vampire jumping over the walls and into the complex. He had looked famished and crazed and Marcus had known immediately he was suffering from the *void*.

Marcus had first seen it a couple of centuries before, in Eastern Europe. The sixteenth century had not been the best for his kind. Vampire hunters were everywhere and towns had imposed early curfews that kept people indoors during the hours of darkness, making it difficult for vampires to find easy prey.

Although many had found ways around it—hunting for prostitutes or vagrants—others had gone hungry. The void took over towns silently but swiftly. As vampires got hungrier, they became more erratic, more violent, less careful. They went anywhere they smelled human blood, no matter the danger involved—just like the rogue vampire who had tried to get into the compound, searching for food.

Marcus had escaped Europe just in time before the big massacre. Vampires were wiped out clean in a matter of weeks, mostly by burning down entire towns and killing everybody suspected of being a vampire—even if they turned out not to be one.

Then something amazing had happened. Over the following few centuries, humans had convinced themselves that vampires weren't real. Quite systematically, they had erased every single detail of the vampire existence from their memory. They simply convinced themselves that it had never happened. Tales of vampires surfaced here and there, mostly in the form of fiction, but it was never taken seriously again. It had given his kind a second chance.

Until last night, when he had come face to face with the void again. It was a sign of how close they all were to becoming desperate. Always just a few meals away from becoming nothing more than animals.

Jaco, the guard who had caught the rogue vampire, was speaking.

"We need to put more guards on the walls, Your Majesty."

Marcus nodded and took a quick look at the walls beyond the window on his right. All walls were at least fifteen feet tall. Too easy for a determined vampire to breach.

"How many?" he asked.

Jaco looked at Miles. "We were thinking at least twice the number we have now."

"Fine. What about the humans?"

"I think we should still keep them away from the outer courtyards. If a rogue happens to make it over a wall, they won't find anybody wandering around."

Miles stepped forward.

"My Lord, the woman…"Every cell in Marcus' body woke up at her mention and his hunger returned with a fury. He turned his gaze towards Miles and his eyes must have screamed "careful" because Miles hesitated for a second.

"Do you want a guard on her?" he said, and Marcus suspected those weren't the words he had intended to say.

A guard. He hadn't told anybody, not even Miles, about Isabelle's immunity to charming—but Miles obviously felt something was amiss, especially given Marcus' sudden interest in taking a pet.

He could appreciate Miles' concern. Miles had been by his side for centuries and they understood each other perfectly. Once upon a time, back in Europe, Miles had saved his life from the hunters. When it came time to flee to America and plan the invasion, he had made sure Miles stayed by his side. Plus, nobody was better than Miles at keeping the compound safe. He had the know-how, but he also had the intuition. A trained warrior with the refined abilities of a vampire.

33

Marcus stood up and walked towards the window. He could see her bedroom from here, but not her. He wished he could will her to the window so he could catch a glimpse of her curves.

"Not yet," he told Miles without turning around. And then the fangs pushed against his gums, claiming to get out. "Give me one night with her first."

He faced away from the window and looked at Jaco. "Get the guards organized for tomorrow. And Miles, get a convoy ready. I want them to go out to look for Patrick."

Miles nodded, a world of questions in his eyes.

"I have a feeling he's planning something big."

CHAPTER 6

The feeling of warmth stretching over her face woke her up. She opened her eyes slowly, adjusting to the brightness. The sun was up, dazzling and strong. The window was open and the air rushing in had a crackly, comforting smell that confused her. The smell of open air, of windows without sealed shutters.

When something popped on the other side of the room, she jumped awake. A fire was slowly dying in the fireplace. There had been no fire when she had gone to bed last night, so somebody had slipped in while she was sleeping and got it going.

A slow sense of panic stirred in the pit of her stomach, making her feel nauseous. Things only got worse as she got up and realized her old clothes were gone. She had taken everything off except a tank top and underwear before going to bed. Now her jeans and jacket, which she had placed on top of a nearby dresser, were no longer there.

She hadn't exactly been expecting privacy or a knock on the door, but she still felt invaded. More than anything, she felt panic at the thought of vampires being so quiet that they could waltz in and out of the room without her even hearing them.

She swallowed hard and only then noticed the lump that had formed in her throat. The last thing she needed was to get paralyzed by fear. It was daylight and she was wasting precious minutes.

She picked some pants, boots and a form-fitting sweater from the closet. Whoever had lived in this room before her had been of similar size and height, because everything fit her almost perfectly. Maybe the king liked a certain kind of woman.

The memory of his lips locked on hers sent her heart into another frenzied dance.

"Damn it," she cursed in a whisper, then shook her head. She needed to concentrate. She also needed food. Her stomach had been growling in protest since the moment she opened her eyes.

Her fingers were trembling with anticipation as she reached for the door's handle, but when she finally opened it, the only thing she found was a deserted courtyard. Walls surrounded the space on three sides, with the massive building closing in on the remaining side. There was a small gate on the opposite wall, and she guessed it led to another inside courtyard. It was a confusing layout and the first thing she needed to do was figure out how big the place was and how far away the exit was.

She stepped into the sun and then turned around to observe the building where her bedroom was. It looked plain but sturdy from the outside, more resembling of a fortress than a place for comfort. The walls appeared to be a mix of stone and brick with a layer of grayish paint on top. Built to last, not to impress, and a far cry from the fanciness of the chandeliers in the king's meeting room.

She crossed the courtyard and reached for the gate, expecting it to be locked. Just like her bedroom's door, it wasn't, even though there was a locking mechanism on it. Either the vampires were very trusting or they had no reason to fear anything or anybody.

A larger courtyard extended on the other side of the gate, similar in format but much more open. She was beginning to think the place was designed like a honeycomb: lots of smaller spaces next to each other, each serving its own purpose and holding a certain number of residents or buildings. Somehow she had been expecting huge open spaces of land with a single tall wall around it—but this was nothing like it.

And then she saw it. Movement, on the far wall, under a long covered corridor. Her heart constricted for a second, then she took off on that direction, nearly running.

A woman about her age was strolling down in the shade. Strolling. Isabelle hadn't seen anybody walk in such a relaxed way for as long as she could remember. Her own walks in the daylight were often half-runs, rushing from one place to the next, trying to cover as much territory as possible before the daylight wore off.

The blonde woman looked directly her way when she heard her steps. Then smiled. A friendly, relaxed smile.

"Hey. I guess you're new."

It was all so casual and relaxed that Isabelle wasn't sure what to say. She had been expecting fear, desperation, people half-malnourished and weak.

"Yeah. I'm Isabelle." She extended her hand and the woman shook it.

"Vicki."

"Where is everybody?"

The woman shrugged. "Oh, here and there."

Isabelle ran her hand through her hair—her hair that felt soft and smelled better than it had in years.

"I guess I was expecting something different. Fear, maybe. But you seem—"

"Content?" Vicki smiled. "I guess I am. You'll find some people here who are scared all the time, but most of us are just glad to not have to run anymore."

"What about them?"

The woman's eyes moved towards her neck. Looking for bite marks.

"I guess you haven't been assigned to anybody yet? Most vampires here are what you would call... civilized. They're not like the ones out on the roads."

A mix of fear and disgust churned Isabelle's stomach. All this time, she had expected to find allies inside the compound. People ready to back her up when the time came. She hadn't considered the possibility that many would be content with their stay there. They had food, they had shelter, they didn't have to live in fear. She guessed that for some, being a slave wasn't so bad if it meant being out of hiding.

"You haven't tried to fight back?" she finally asked, even though she knew the answer.

Vicki looked at her like she was crazy. "Fight back? With what? And why? Nobody forced me to come here."

Isabelle's eyes flew towards the massive walls and the gate connecting to what she suspected was another courtyard. "So the gates are unlocked?"

"No. But they'll unlock them for you if you want to leave."

Isabelle stood still for a second, trying to understand what the woman was saying.

"At night? You can only leave at night?"

The woman's smile disappeared. "I don't think you understand. Nobody here wants to leave. The monsters out there are the real monsters."

~*~

It wasn't until she got to the kitchen area—after crossing a labyrinth of corridors and smaller courtyards—that she started to realize what the woman had meant. There was food everywhere. Cupboards of everything from cereal to dry fruits to staples ready to be used for cooking. Even more impressive was the fridge, holding not only icy water, but also meats and fruits. She had a million questions as to how those things had gotten there, though she guessed the vampires had their own scavenging parties in order to find food and keep the humans alive. And because they didn't have to worry about being hunted while on the road, they could stay out for days, reaching farther destinations and discovering better treasures.

She tried all the drawers and couldn't find a single knife. Forks and spoons were everywhere, but it wasn't like you could do much damage with either of those. She finally grabbed a couple of fruits and sat down at the kitchen table, trying to figure out what to do next.

Vicki had said there were at least a hundred humans in the compound. Isabelle expected at least some of them to be unhappy about their arrangement—or at least she hoped so. Still, if it came to a fight, she wondered whether the people there would side with her—or with those they thought had the better chance of winning.

The monsters out there are the real monsters, the woman had said. Was she trying to say that the monsters inside were less than terrible?

Isabelle's mind flew back to the king, warm and alive against her body. To the world of sensations a simple kiss had awakened. She could feel a ripple separating her body from her mind—one pulling towards him, wanting more, the other reminding her he was the reason humanity was almost gone. The line separating the two was so distinct, so clear, yet she was having trouble staying on the right side of it.

She had been expecting him to come into her bedroom the night before. To get into her bed without a single word, like an animal taking over the very thing he had power over. She had expected pain, blood and violence. But he never came—and part of her had been disappointed. The realization that she wanted him was eerie and more than a little troubling. More so because she knew he hadn't been able to charm her, which meant that everything she had felt was just hers. No mind tricks, no illusions—just raw sensation spreading through her body like a powerful wave.

It scared her.

The tap of steps behind her caught her by surprise and made her jump.

"Sorry, didn't mean to scare you," Vicki said. "You're still a little jumpy."

Isabelle nodded. "Living in hiding would do that to you. Where is everybody?"

Vicki grabbed a glass of cold water and sat next to her.

"Sleeping, mostly. After you've been here for a while, you start living on their schedule. It just makes more sense."

Nothing here made sense to her, but she didn't want to argue. "Why aren't you?"

"I like the silence of the daytime, so I try to stay awake when I can. Are you waiting to be assigned to somebody?"

Ripples of sensations looped through her body, reaching down to her stomach. "I'm pretty sure I've been assigned already."

Vicki frowned. "They usually bite you on the neck the first time."

Usually? She suddenly felt nauseous and pushed the half-eaten apple away from her.

"How is it, when they're…?"

"Inside you? You're half asleep by the time they do that. Or maybe asleep is not the right term. You're just… not really there. The spell or whatever it is they do to you, it puts you in sort of a trance. Makes you mellow and soft. So your body is going through the motions but your mind is not really there."

Isabelle stirred in the chair.

"Why? I mean, couldn't they do it without charming you?"

Vicki raised her left arm and pointed to a large bruise.

"Things get… rough sometimes. This is the only way we're not completely panicking all the time."

And Isabelle decided she didn't want to know any more details.

~*~

She spent the next three hours exploring every corner of the complex. Most buildings contained either bedrooms or random rooms that didn't seem to serve any specific purpose. Some rooms were oddly shaped, as if they were originally meant to have a door or window somewhere—but somebody had decided at the very last minute not to put it there. She guessed the layout would get less confusing after a few days, but it still seemed like an odd design choice.

A lot of the corridors led nowhere and so did many rooms. You would step into a space expecting to reach the room behind it, but there would be no way to move between the two rooms—except to walk outside and around the building to reach another door. It seemed like a very odd architectural choice. The corridors were even stranger. You would exit the last door on the wall and see the corridor continue for twenty feet or more until it reached a dead end. There were no other doors, exits or even objects in the remaining corridor space. Just empty space leading nowhere.

Maybe it was meant to be a metaphor for the humans in there: here's your freedom, you're going nowhere anyway.

By late afternoon, she had decided to go back to the building where her bedroom was. It wasn't only the largest of all the buildings—it was also the only one that had a number of locked doors. In fact, hers was the only room she could access in the entire section of the building. From outside, it seemed like a massive construction. At least two floors and several rooms deep. Her bedroom opened up to the courtyard but so did other rooms—except that all of them were inaccessible. The only other door in her bedroom was also locked. She'd thought that maybe it led to his bedroom, but it could also be a way into the rest of the building. Either way, she couldn't get through.

She was missing something. She had to be.

As the sun went down, she witnessed the compound rise again. Lights sprang to life here and there, revealing eyes shining from dark corners. Whispers spread through the corridors and the sounds intensified. The human sounds. She could spot the vampires moving around, their eyes glowing in the night, but she never heard them. They moved quietly, graciously, as if the world around them didn't exist. Or as if they could move without disturbing the air around them.

She talked to a few more people, but decided not to ask any important questions. Too many eyes spying from the darkness, too many questions as to where everybody's loyalty lay.

The compound was a different world at night, but something still remained true: she wasn't ready to trust anybody, human or not.

CHAPTER 7

Marcus cursed as he opened the window into the night. He'd been restless all day, unable to sleep. Isabelle had been on his thoughts, flashes of her heartbeat and her lips looping in his mind.

It had been a long time since a woman had kept him awake. Whatever made Isabelle immune to his charming also made her irresistible. His hunger spread, ached inside him. A hunger that was more than just physical. He wanted to possess her, own her. He wondered if that was what Patrick felt when he attacked his victims without charming them. The feeling of victory as you took over and completely owned somebody.

Except that Marcus didn't want to hurt Isabelle. He wanted to claim her as his, to keep her close.

It was a new and surprising discovery. Humans usually bored him. They were too attached to petty feelings, too scared all the time. When the invasion began, he had expected resistance. Not only from the government and the military—which he'd gotten—but from everyday people as well. Humans who were ready to fight and die to protect their freedom. But except for small pockets of resistance here and there, his army had found little fight in humans. And the lack of a fight had made it easier for vampires like Patrick to go on a killing rampage.

While part of him had been relieved about how quickly they'd been able to take over, there had been a small spark of disappointment in him too. He'd felt robbed. After centuries of seeing the best and the worst of humans, he wanted a fight. He wanted vindication for the years of hunting and persecution. Instead, he'd gotten weakness. Although the military had fought hard, they were unprepared and outnumbered. In the end, surprise had won over brute force. Short of bombing every city, the military had no other weapon against vampires. So he made sure they were disposed of quickly, before they could reassemble their troops somewhere else and try again.

He wondered if Isabelle would have the fire to fight back. She was at the compound, so part of her had given up—or at least appeared to.

But she had also braved the roads on her own to make it there. She had probably even braved the night.

Maybe before he took her to bed, he needed to ask her some questions.

$$-*-$$

When Miles first showed up to get her, she had a million questions. It didn't take long to see he wasn't going to answer any of them. Part of her wanted to talk about anything, even the weather—just to keep her mind away from the king and what might be waiting for her in his room.

She had been ready for it before she came to the compound. She knew what being a pet entailed and she had told herself she would do it. Quietly and without raising any questions.

That was before she met the king. Now her stomach was tied up in knots and all she could think about was whether she would panic when things started happening. And if she did panic, how would she handle it, since he wouldn't be able to calm her down?

That was another question running circles around her mind. She'd realized the day before that he couldn't charm her. She wasn't sure how common that was or what it really meant for her. It had surprised the king, at least—and Miles' eyes seemed particularly intense on her today, as if he was trying to will her to do something. She didn't quite understand how charming worked, whether she would "hear" the command in her mind or simply become compliant and respond to anything they'd ask. Whatever it was, she wasn't feeling it.

"Are you ready?" Miles asked, holding the door open.

She was nowhere ready, but she nodded yes anyway.

Part of her was terrified of what was coming. The other part couldn't wait for the king's hands to touch her again. It was a strange mix of emotions—and a very unexpected one.

But it was something she'd been preparing for for months and turning back was no longer an option.

~*~

Before he even stepped out of the shadows, her heart was already racing.

As soon as she walked into his room, he picked up the beating of her heart. Alive and full of fire. Her eyes darted around the room, settling on the bed for a few extra seconds before returning to him. It was a bed made for pleasure: ample, soft, inviting—and she seemed to appreciate it. The look in her eyes caused his body to react, the urge of his hunger rearing up his call again.

She looked stunning and she smelled even better. The aroma of her blood and her skin mixed into the air, making his fangs ache. His whole body wanted to jump on her right then and there and push her down onto the ground. It was an animal urge that was hard to ignore—and one he wasn't used to feeling. Not because he was immune to that kind of feeling, but because when you lived for centuries, you learned to control your urges.

Isabelle was one urge that was proving difficult to control. Good thing he wasn't planning on controlling it for long.

He pointed at the large couch across from the bed. "Sit down, Isabelle."

Pushing his hunger down, he tried to concentrate on her eyes. They were the color of a stormy sea: blue and gray all rolled into one. And at the moment, a storm was raging in them. It was obvious she was on edge—and he would've loved to be able to read her mind to see what exactly was causing it. Was it fear or excitement? He could guess it was a bit of both—but he desperately wanted to know which emotion was winning.

"Where did you come from, Isabelle?"

The words came out softly, almost casual, but the heat built up inside him. He was more edgy around her than he should have been.

"East," she said, and he could immediately tell she was lying.

He sat down on the other end of the couch and her heart sped up. Not only could he hear it, he could smell the rush of adrenaline in her blood. His eyes moved down towards her chest, almost as an acknowledgment. Her face reddened, the heat radiating out of her body and hitting him like a wave. His whole body groaned in response.

Control yourself, damn it. "Did you spend the night on the road?"

A slight shiver ran through her body. "Yes, inside an abandoned factory."

His brow furrowed, his eyes firm and locked into hers. "Did you run into any of us?"

She hesitated for a second before she nodded yes. *What are you hiding, Isabelle?*

He wondered if she could see the mix of emotions in his eyes. "How did they look?"

"I only saw one up close," she said, stirring on the couch. "He looked powerful, scary."

He didn't want to get the questions out, have to explain what the void was. But he needed to know. "Did he look famished?"

Isabelle swallowed hard. "I'm not sure I understand…"

He inched closer, his heat spreading like a raging fire towards her.

"The one you got a chance to see up close, did he look rabid, like an animal?"

Her body froze. When she opened her mouth, her voice came out shaky. "No, he… he was smooth and calm."

It was taking all of his strength not to grab her right at that moment. No, not grab her. Pounce on her. Just like a big cat bringing the prey down. He didn't want to scare her, but he wasn't sure that he could control himself much longer. Her heart was hammering in her chest and every beat felt like an invitation.

~*~

Her whole body was pulsating and so was her mind. As he moved closer, she felt herself slipping from reality, everything around her melting away. Until all that was left were those silver eyes and the heat of his body drifting into hers.

Those eyes. They were silvery black in the darkness of the room. They had been a deep grey the night before, but they seemed to have a light of their own that night. They didn't look like the eyes of a predator. They looked inviting and... safe. She knew it didn't make sense but his proximity was the closest thing to safety she had felt in a long time. No looking over her shoulder, not cringing away at the sounds of the night. She clenched her hands, trying to push the feeling away.

"Were you afraid of him?"

Her heart thumped loudly in her eardrums. "I was terrified."

And then he was so close she could actually feel his breath on her lips. It was causing the electricity of the room to intensify—but it also felt like velvet spilling over her skin. He smelled like the Earth: salt and musk and wood.

His eyes were locked on hers. "Are you afraid of me?"

"No."

There it was, the real answer. She had been asking herself that exact question since the moment she saw him. Was she afraid of him? Would she be once he got close, once she knew there was nowhere to run? And the truth was that she wasn't. The king inspired a very different, more powerful emotion in her. Something that completely erased any hint of fear that could have been lurking around. Something that made her forget who he was and who she was and why every hint of desire clutching at her should have felt so wrong.

Even though it felt deliciously right.

The silver in his eyes seemed to spark brighter as one of his hands extended towards her, slightly brushing her cheek before settling on the back of her neck.

"I'm not afraid of you," she repeated, more to savor the revelation than to reassure him.

And then his mouth reached for hers and her mind went blank.

A soft moan escaped her throat as soon as his lips touched hers. It was a sound of wanting but also of surrender. She wanted this. Her body craved it, but so did something deeper inside of her, something that was waking up with every passing second.

She was expecting a hard invasion, but he didn't push. Instead, his lips were soft, testing and tasting. The silky caress was so erotic, her whole body turned to liquid, melting into his. More, she needed more. She moaned against his mouth and her lips opened.

And then all of a sudden the gentleness was gone. His tongue darted into her mouth, twining with hers, demanding a response, while his hands ran down her ribs and towards her lower back.

One of his hands reached for her waist, sliding her under him. As he leaned over her, every inch of skin he touched went up in flames, warmth extending inwards and spreading like wildfire. Part of her mind was desperately trying to hold on to reason, reminding her over and over that he wasn't human.

Except the things he was making her body feel were all very human.

His hand moved under her shirt and her whole body trembled as if hit by an electrical current. His touch was hypnotic. So wrong and yet so right. She arched against him, begging for more.

He growled in response and moved his hand higher, reaching for her breast.

Before his fingers touched her nipple, it had already hardened. When he finally touched her, he let a groan out and pushed harder into her mouth. He sucked on her tongue and she found herself falling deeper into the darkness, into him. Nothing mattered at the moment. Not her mission, not her hate for the monsters. All that mattered was his hands and his tongue dancing with hers. Because nothing she had ever felt, nobody she had ever touched, had felt like this.

Then all of a sudden, he broke the kiss. A moan of complaint left her throat and she reached for his mouth, but he pulled back. She opened her eyes, searching for an explanation—and found his eyes locked on hers, bright silver and deep.

"Marcus," he groaned, his chest rising up and down rapidly.

She tried to make sense through the fog of desire clogging up her mind. Her head was spinning and it was hard to concentrate on anything but his scent and his heat, dancing over her body.

"What?"

"My name is Marcus. Say it."

She pushed against him.

"Marcus," she whispered and the hum of his name on her lips felt like honey.

He growled, the sound rolling over her like thunder. His hands felt feverish against her skin and she could see the transformation happening in him. As the touch became more urgent, he slowly let go of his hold on humanity. His eyes darkened, his fangs came out and the rhythm of his movements became more animal, more dominant. He pressed harder, moved harder, pinching and stroking and kneading until pain started to inch closer.

Hot, delicious pain encircling her body

She gasped as he pinched her nipple, ripples of pain and pleasure shooting through her. She knew she should feel afraid, but the changes only served to intensify what she was feeling. She wanted more.

Marcus' eyes met hers. "Still not scared, Belle?"

"No," she growled, out of breath.

That seemed to be the signal he'd been waiting for, because as soon as she spoke, he reached for the buttons of her shirt. He moved painfully slow, savoring each inch of skin revealed and each of her moans along with it. When her shirt was off, he pulled the bra off in a single move, without even touching the clasp. Then a hint of a smile showed on his face, a small trace of the beast reaching through his eyes and waiting to devour her. Her entire body melted.

She opened her lips to say something, although she wasn't sure what. Before any words formed, his mouth was back on hers, teasing and nibbling while his hands continued undressing her. The mix of sensations rushing through her veins felt like liquid fire. It was need and hunger and desire all mixed into one.

Whispers slipped in between kisses. "You taste good, Belle."

He did too. The taste of the forbidden, of raw heat devouring everything in his path. And she wanted more of it.

She opened her hazed eyes and realized his shirt was gone. Her hands instinctively reached for his skin. Black ink curled down one of his sides into an intricate pattern of what seemed like letters. Some ancient symbol she couldn't understand. As she stretched forward to touch him, she felt drunk, hypnotized—and she knew at once she was lost. Her hand touched the tattoo, then moved over his stomach. The second her fingers landed there, he moaned. He was all stone: hard and chiseled to perfection. Ripples of muscle waved and coiled under her touch. She slid her hands downward towards the waistline of his pants, groaning when she encountered the fabric blocking her.

"Please, I want to touch you," she said, and her own voice sounded low and hoarse.

He moved away without speaking, stripping off the last remaining items of clothing. As he slid his pants down, Belle's eyes grew bigger. He was magnificent, all rough and tense, a mix of human perfection and supernatural beast. He was large and more than ready—and a pang of delightful fear pulsed between her legs.

She wanted to be devoured. Consumed. Her eyes moved up and she saw a hint of fangs showing through his half-open lips. Her throat seemed to throb in response and he must have noticed it, because he grunted.

Then he leaned down, pressing his body over hers. When his cock pushed against her thigh, her whole body bucked in response, arching against him.

"I can't wait to taste you," he groaned against her lips and she wasn't sure if he meant taste her blood or taste her sex. The idea of either one made her core throb with anticipation.

His mouth trailed over her neck, his fangs grazing the skin and taunting her. The touch was like nothing she had ever felt. Forbidden and lustful and nearly desperate. Her body was on edge, straining to stay in control and slowly losing the battle. He was innately powerful and she felt herself slowly letting go of her defenses, wanting to be taken, held down, possessed. Wanting to feel his power.

When his lower body pushed against her, shifting thighs further apart, her head lolled back in response.

His mouth closed over her neck, licking and sucking and tasting until she realized he was making her want his bite. Barely aware of the pleading sounds she was making, she moved against him, her hips pushing against his erection.

Before she realized he had moved, his mouth was down on her breast, his teeth nibbling on the nipple gently. A shot of wild pleasure reached in, her body growing tighter and wetter. The pulsing between her legs got stronger, aching for release. She wondered if he could smell her desire, raw and demanding. Almost as if responding to the questions, he sucked on her nipple harder, his tongue dancing and teasing.

Her nails dug into his back in response and he looked up. The darkness of his eyes was deep and exquisite and all she wanted was to get lost in them. Reach into his soul and see what lurked there. What secrets he held, what things he'd seen. Without looking away, he reached down with one hand, trailing down her stomach and towards her thigh.

When his fingers reached between her legs, her breathing froze.

Oh, God, she thought, but the thought dissolved away almost immediately, because then he pushed a finger inside her and a stroke of what felt like lightning shook her body. He pushed in further, adding another finger and then another, rocking his hand against her wetness. Tight, so tight. Every inch of her body was pulsing with arousal.

He moaned along with her as he pressed his fingers inside her. And suddenly his fingers were gone from inside her and his hands were clutching her legs open. He slid down between her legs and her hands curled over the sides of the couch, holding on to whatever edge she could find.

His tongue burned a trail over her abdomen and then up and down her thigh. He stopped right before reaching her sex and she groaned in protest.

When his tongue finally lapped at her, slow and lingering, her mind unraveled. It was absolutely delirious and it melted away any remaining thoughts about who she was, who he was and how wrong this pleasure was supposed to feel. Because it felt exquisite and she had no choice but to let herself be swallowed by the feeling. With each wave of pleasure, her own climax built, growling in her stomach like a wild animal clamoring to break free.

His lips closed over her clit, sucking gently, and she clutched at his shoulders. Pulling and grabbing, asking for more the only way she could. She wanted him inside her, filling her, owning her. Even if she was betraying everything and everybody she loved because of it.

He looked up as if he'd heard her thoughts. "I want to be inside you now," he said, his voice husky and low. All she could do was nod among the sounds of pleasure escaping her throat.

Sliding back over her body, he steadied himself between her legs. All the nerve endings in her body were pulsing, igniting in urgency. A mix of her heartbeat and his was throbbing in her ears.

The tip of his cock pushed against her and she gasped. He was huge and as he pushed slowly inside her, she felt her muscles stretch around him. The pain was exquisite.

"You're so tight," he groaned and pushed an inch deeper.

The slow invasion was driving her insane. She moaned and moved against him, working her hips to make the invasion easier. That seemed to undo his self-control, because he grabbed her ass and with a single, grinding thrust, he rammed into her.

She gasped in both surprise and agony. Her muscles pulsed around his length as he remained still, packed taut inside her, giving her time to get used to his size. She felt full, heavy, possessed.

His face was tight, a look of restraint washing over his features. He was holding back the beast—and she suddenly, desperately want him to let it out.

She moved against him and he growled in response. The pressure in her belly coiled and tightened. *Move, please move,* she thought.

And then he did. Not in the slow rhythm she was expecting, but in one hard, deep thrust. She arched against him, her neck open and inviting. He rammed into her again as he bent down over her. Blood was roaring in her ears, deafening and hot. When his mouth got closer to her neck, she felt the feverish cadence of her heart concentrating there. Her entire body quivered as he pounded into her once more before his teeth pierced the soft skin of her neck.

There was a brief moment of pain, but as soon as he started to suck, her body exploded into waves of pleasure. The orgasm sent swirling coils of pleasure over her skin and deep into her, her body crumpling in a sea of ecstasy. Her muscles clenched around him and he sucked harder, fire scorching her skin where his mouth was.

Her moan was deep, primitive, and it sent him into a frenzy. He moved his lips away and pumped faster, like a beast searching for release. He pounded harder, feverish. She opened her eyes and through the daze of pleasure, she saw his face transforming. Raw, animal power defining his features. The black in his eyes was deep, as if a storm of darkness was raging in them. His fangs were out, a drop of her blood still coating his lips.

Her eyes lingered on it, mesmerized. He seemed to catch the heavy sight of pleasure in her gaze and bent over to kiss her, the metallic taste of blood mixing with her saliva. A second orgasm rippled through her as his tongue tangled with hers, the wave of pleasure making her gasp for air.

She clanged to him as the waves of the orgasm rippled through her, making her soar higher than she'd thought possible. As her muscles pulsed around his length, he responded by grunting and pounding harder into her body, reaching so deep her insides trembled with the invasion.

She opened her eyes and saw the tightness in his jaw, the fire of his eyes burning deep into hers. She pushed into his hips hard, demanding, holding his pleasure tight and pulling until she thought he couldn't take it any longer. And then he exploded inside her. He grabbed her ass and pumped into her one more time, grunting as he released, arching his back as a howl of pleasure erupted from his throat.

When his face came down to stare at her, there was a flash of rapture in his eyes. Satisfaction. She wasn't sure if it was a look of possession or a look of abandonment. Either way, it tore down into her, making her body tingle with something that felt like bliss.

She felt exhausted, sleep washing over her and grabbing her until she felt weak and sluggish. Her limbs were soft, trembling still with the aftershocks of the climax. And as she fell asleep, her mind blissfully softening into the night, she heard him get up and leave the room. Before sleep overtook her, she heard his command to one of the guards.

"Find out who she is."

CHAPTER 8

She woke up slower than usual the next morning. Her body was spent and sluggish, a heaviness washing over her. Part of her also felt warm and comforted, though, and that was somewhat more unsettling considering what had brought it on.

The sounds of the morning were filtering in through the half-open window, slowly lifting her drowsiness. Her mind was a blur of cluttered ideas and trying to make sense of them was almost impossible. She opened her eyes slowly, taking her surroundings in one detail at a time. She was in his room. Alone.

The memories of the previous night rolled over her, like waves crashing against the sand. Each crash brought with it a new flash of skin, of pleasure, of fire on fire exploding. She was a traitor. It had taken one touch, one second of his lips on hers to forget everything. Even though she had known from the beginning that sleeping with a vampire was part of the deal, she hadn't expected to enjoy it. The pleasure had been the greatest treason of all.

She shifted on the bed and her muscles ached. It was the kind of glorious pain that a wild night could bring. Only that in this case, it felt like something more. Her body seemed different. *Branded.* She reached for her neck and the two puncture wounds there. They were barely noticeable but they were there—like a brand. *You're mine.* Marcus' words looped in her mind, bringing a shiver with them every time she heard them again.

She took a deep breath and sat upright. Her biggest distress wasn't about the marks on her neck. It was about something deeper. Somehow, her soul felt marked. Last night hadn't been about passion or sex or blood. It had been about surrendering—and she had done it. Completely and without reservations. And the consequences of that terrified her, because suddenly she was having second thoughts.

Maybe the king wasn't such a monster.

Maybe she didn't need to kill him.

Except that there was no other way out. And that realization was paralyzing. He was the king of the monsters. He was also Marcus, the one who had made her body sing the night before. She could feel a war starting between her heart and her mind, so she decided to get up and stop thinking about it for a while. Or at least try.

There was something else nagging at the back of her mind: the word rabid. She'd had little time to think about it last night because Marcus' kiss had erased everything else from her mind. But now the word was back, sending chills down her spine. *Rabid.*

She'd never seen any vampire who would fit the description, so she had no idea what Marcus had meant. Up until the day before she had never even come face to face with a vampire. She had seen them exploring the surroundings, hunting for blood—but she had never had the chance to exchange words with one. But even from the distance, they had always looked graceful to her. They had a certain *quality* to their movements, a touch of regality that humans lacked. A few times she had found herself almost hypnotized by their movements.

When the invasion first began, many had tried to deny the reality of what was happening. The news spent the first few hours reporting the attacks as mass hysteria and just a few isolated incidents of violence. She suspected that the government had tried to keep things hush-hush to avoid panic, but what they created instead was a nation unprepared to fight. By the time the invasion was obvious, civilization had run out of chances to do anything about it.

Her first close encounter with a vampire had been in the hospital. She had been doing her intern rounds in the ER when an ambulance rushed in. The victim was barely moving and she was incredibly white, but it wasn't until they started working on her that they had realized the problem: she had barely any blood left in her body. Massive blood loss usually meant a considerable injury, but the woman had no visible injuries, except for a small set of puncture marks on her left wrist.

And that was when she'd seen him. In the frantic running around, she had lifted her eyes for a second and seen the vampire standing a few feet away. His eyes had shone bright as he watched the doctors work on the woman. There was a subtle buzzing of energy around him, almost as if he was affecting the electricity of the room by just standing there. Now she would never mistake his poised movements for anything else, but back then, she wasn't yet convinced of the existence of vampires. So she stood in place, distracted for a second by the stranger's unrelenting look.

When the machine finally beeped a flatline, he had turned around and left.

That first image had always defined her view of vampires: cool, unmovable. And dangerously alluring.

The idea of a rabid vampire, acting deranged and thrashing around like an animal, seemed unthinkable. So why had Marcus mentioned it? And what exactly were they?

Because if there was something else out there, something she didn't know about, it meant the people back at the house didn't know it either. And history had proven that ignorance would get you killed.

So before she signed her own death sentence by trying to kill the king, she needed to figure out what the world was really up against.

~*~

Marcus looked towards the blackened window and a pang of irritation hit him. The sun was up and he was still awake. This was the second day in a row that sleep had evaded him and he wasn't happy about it. In fact, he was pretty annoyed about the whole thing. Now on top of having to deal with the threat of the rabid vampires and the void spreading, he also had a woman dancing in his mind.

It was an unsettling mix of emotions. For a vampire who had been around for centuries, it was also a startling discovery knowing a human had such power over him. He wouldn't have minded so much if he had some way of controlling the situation, but Isabelle was way beyond his reach.

He paced, moving away from the window and towards the door that separated his studio from his bedroom. He heard a ripple in the air coming from the adjoining room and knew Isabelle was awake. It was just a small crackle, the sound of skin brushing against fabric—but it was enough to tell him she was up and moving. His stomach contracted and he cursed. He wanted—needed—more time with her. There was something about Isabelle that called him. It was a sort of electric hum that spread down to his bones and awoke his hunger. Something he'd never experienced with a human before.

Something he hadn't experienced in a very long time.

There hadn't been any female vampires for over four centuries. When the void had spread, it had had a devastating effect on the female side of his breed. Female vampires became erratic and violent much faster and much sooner—not only against humans but also against other vampires. Many were killed by their own partners in an attempt to crush the spreading plague. In less than a year, every single female vampire had been infected with the void and died—either of hunger or at the hands of other vampires.

Back then, many had turned to keeping human pets as a way to fight the loneliness. He had tried it too, but had quickly realized it wasn't what he wanted. Humans were fragile and always terrified. The physical pleasure he got from them did little for his mind and his soul. What he wanted was a partner, an equal—and humans had never been able to reach that level.

Against all reason, he was now wondering whether Isabelle could.

The question had been in his mind since the moment he first realized she was immune to charming. But after last night, the question had become a lot stronger. A lot more real.

What if?

His body tensed and he had to shake his head to let go of the thought. Suddenly, he was glad he was alone and didn't have to explain his emotions to Miles or anybody else who knew him well. It wasn't hard to imagine what their reactions would be.

The king taking a human companion.

It wasn't forbidden or impossible, but it was surely unheard of—and it made him uneasy. But thinking about it also sent his heart into a race and that was enough to tell him there was something there.

Of course, he knew little about Isabelle besides the fact that he couldn't charm her. He knew she was passionate and strong. He knew that in bed, she was already his equal. Whether she could be the same outside of the bedroom was a question to ponder.

A knock on the opposite side of the room startled him. The compound was built over a long series of underground tunnels that stretched for miles. They connected all the important rooms inside the compound to each other and allowed his kind to move around without being exposed to sunlight. He remembered a time when daylight meant hiding away in cellars and caves—and he had made sure no hiding was necessary when he built the compound.

"Come in, Miles," he said without approaching the hidden door.

A panel on the wall slid open and Miles walked in. His face was somber, tight.

"What is it?"

Despite the grave eyes, Miles seemed calm and collected. But then, Miles always looked that way. It was the reason Marcus had appointed him to deal with security. Miles was immovable. Not because he didn't have emotions, but because he never let them affect him. At least not visibly.

"The first patrol group came back," Miles told him. "They found a few rabids."

"How far?"

"A couple of hours away," Miles said. "They've never been this close before."

Marcus slid into the chair facing his bedroom door. Isabelle could've run into one of them out there—and so could the other humans trying to reach the compound. While there was enough blood in the compound, the supply was low everywhere else around the country. He couldn't risk losing humans to the rabids out there. On the other hand, he knew that the less the rabids fed, the faster the void would spread. It was a losing proposition either way.

He turned towards Miles, searching for answers. "How worried are you?"

Miles frowned. "More than I was six months ago."

Marcus' heart thumped against his ribs. "What about the guards?"

"They're on the walls since last night. But if a group of rabids attacks—"

"I know," he interrupted. "It'll be a nasty fight."

"We'll spread the word throughout the compound tonight. Tell the humans to stay away from the outer walls."

"How much time do you think we have?"

Miles moved closer. "Can I speak freely, sir?"

Marcus nodded. If there was somebody he could count on telling him the truth, it was Miles. They were as close as brothers. "Of course."

"If the void keeps spreading, we'll be outnumbered soon."

Marcus knew it.

"How's the research going?"

Miles shook his head slightly. "Nothing new, I'm afraid, but I was thinking… the new woman…"

Marcus' whole body tensed up.

"There's something different about her," Miles continued. "Maybe we can…"

"No."

He could feel his own eyes darkening as he looked at Miles.

"Nobody is touching her except me," he said softly, but the words burned their way up his throat.

Miles stood quiet, not a single muscle moving.

"Understood," he finally said.

"Make sure everybody's aware of this, Miles," Marcus said. "If we ever come under attack, her safety comes first. Are we clear?"

Miles' face was a perfectly-carved piece of stone.

"Yes, sir."

As he was leaving, Miles turned around to face the king just one last time. "Marcus?"

The king looked up and saw the concern in his friend's expression.

"I'll be careful, Miles."

Miles nodded, then stepped through the secret door and disappeared into the labyrinth of tunnels.

Nothing was going as Marcus had expected. When he had put the team of scientists together—the "great vampire minds," Miles had called them—he had been hoping for a much faster resolution. He'd even sent a team around the country to collect the best lab equipment they could find—and that hadn't been an easy task, considering the state of ruin of everything around them.

And still, they had nothing.

Coming up with a blood substitute had proven a lot more difficult than the scientists had expected. They were close—or so they kept saying—but they couldn't nail the right combination of chemicals and nutrients. Or when they did, they couldn't figure out how to keep the blood "alive" for more than just a few minutes.

Time was running short—especially now that the rabids were getting closer. When he'd first started the lab, the only thing he had had in mind was making sure everybody could feed even if humans disappeared. At the rate they were being killed during the invasion, it had been a very real possibility that they would become extinct someday. Now he was wondering whether having a blood substitute could stop the void from spreading. And whether the rabids could be turned back if given enough blood. He didn't know if that had ever been attempted before. After all, it made more sense to just abandon or destroy the vampires who became rabid—or at least it had made sense centuries ago, when science could not have attempted to come up with a cure.

If there was a chance for his plan to work, though, it had to happen soon. He could feel the rabids closing in on him.

CHAPTER 9

She had spent most of the day thinking about him and what happened the night before. Replaying the skin and the kisses and the fire over and over again. Until she felt like she was about to go insane if she didn't find a way to press pause on the movie playing in her head.

So she'd kept herself busy by exploring the courtyards and trying to make sense of the layout of the place. Figuring out the connections of the different sections and where each door led gave her a headache, so she ended up returning to the memories of the previous night over and over.

By the time Miles came to get her, she was going insane with anticipation.

The minute she got back into Marcus' room and saw the outline of his form in the darkness, a weight lifted and she could finally relax. She let out a sigh and immediately realized she'd been half-breathing the entire day.

"You can sit down, Belle."

Belle. The nickname sounded like music on his lips.

She found a plush sofa and sat down. *God, he's beautiful.* In the semi-darkness of the room, his eyes almost sparkled. Every time he moved, the ripples in his muscles flexed and tensed up. Flashes of skin against skin looped through her mind.

She blushed and he groaned in response.

"Stop it," he whispered. "I can hear your heart from here."

She took a deep breath and tried to steady the beating in her chest. Then he got closer to sit on the couch and her heart went on a frenzied dash again.

Damn it.

"You have no idea how tempting that sound is," he said.

It was taking all of her willpower not to move closer. Judging by the tightness in his neck and shoulders, it was obvious he was feeling the same.

"I need to talk to you," he said. It sounded almost like a complaint.

She nodded, mainly because she wasn't sure she could actually speak without moaning in the process.

Before she even realized what she was doing, she licked her lips. Marcus groaned and frantically reached for her, his mouth closing on hers. There was none of the gentle touch of the night before. No exploring or waiting for a reaction.

Without breaking the kiss, he picked her up and moved her over to the bed. She felt weightless in his arms, her mind reeling in his power. She wasn't sure how it happened, but most of their clothes were off in seconds. His scent, earthly and otherworldly all mixed into one, washed over her. It was intoxicating and she had to catch her breath because she felt like falling, sliding quickly into a dark abyss of fire and craving.

His mouth reached for her breast, then slid down her body, leaving branding marks everywhere he touched, searing, scorching heat taking over until it hurt. Until she wanted to cry out in desperation, begging for more.

His lips and his tongue moved over the inside of her thighs, teasing and tasting. With one finger, he reached down and pulled the elastic of her underwear off, the last remaining item of clothing between them gone. Then he slid the finger to rest over her swollen clit, starting a slow circling motion. Her gasp reached towards him like a wave, enticing and feverish. She could feel his hunger reaching out in return, pulling, demanding satisfaction. The craving of the beast, hammering to get out and take what it needed. What it craved.

He had an effect on her that she couldn't explain. Once he touched her, any sense of control in her shattered, ramped-up ache and need consuming her.

The combination of his tongue and his fingers on her were driving her insane. When his tongue circled her clit and then plunged into her, she bucked into him. It was too much. Everything about him was too much. The intensity of his touch, the way he seemed to enjoy her taste, the longing he awoke in her.

Then his fangs grazed the skin of her thigh and her whole body stirred. The groan that came out of his throat in response was so guttural, so basic and primitive, it shook her to the core.

Teeth reached higher, following a trail up her thigh until they reached the throbbing pulse of a vein. Right at the crease of her thigh, so she could almost feel his breath rolling over the swollen lips of her sex. She let out a moan and he growled in response, sending delicious waves of heat up and into her, filling her and driving her insane with lust.

His teeth pressed just a little harder and the sensation was so erotic, she couldn't hold back a cry. The realization of what he was about to do hit her just a couple of seconds before his fangs pierced her skin. He sucked on the blood flowing out, grunting as he savored the warmth of the liquid rushing in.

A flash of agonizing pleasure ripped through her body, the orgasm hitting her hard and unexpectedly. As she was coming, waves of pleasure ripping through her, he moved in between her legs and rammed into her. She was pulsing from the orgasm and the invasion felt on the edge of painful. Lusciously painful and breaching and *oh-so-amazing*. Her muscles clenched around him, holding on tight.

"I've never wanted anybody this much, Belle," he said and the words dug into her with unexpected force, reaching for her mind, for her soul. "Seeing you come drives me insane."

Her core tightened as the words rippled over her. She thought it wasn't possible for her to come again, but then he pumped harder into her and something stirred, feeding the hunger and making her entire body shiver. He was so big and so deep inside her, she felt stretched, invaded. Taken.

He moved again, grunting every time he rocked his hips against her. His beautiful features were taut with restraint, a predatory glimmer over his cheekbones and the tight curve of his neck. He was holding back, trying to maintain control. And she desperately wanted him to let loose, to be so overcome with the fire that he couldn't think, couldn't do anything except pound into her.

She pushed into him, her hips deepening the invasion, stretching her more. He grew bigger, tighter, hotter, both inside her and over her skin. His control frayed, edged over the abyss. Then he opened his eyes and looked at her, a current of heat crackling between them, irradiating with such intensity, she could almost feel her skin smoldering.

"I want you to come again, Belle," he grunted, then rammed inside her again.

The words made her gasp, tension and need building higher until she was moaning along with him.

He grabbed her thighs, holding her against him as he pounded harder and more feverishly. Reaching so deep she thought she might break. And then she wished would increase the pressure, the soreness, the delicious torture building inside her.

"Marcus… please, more," she purred, her head heavy with the buzz of hunger and need.

A flash of darkness crossed over his face, making her moan. He reached down to kiss her, a hint of violence in the tongue invading her mouth. He tasted so real, so humanly raw. He growled into her mouth, the edges of his control blurring away.

And then the threads of her desire snapped and she came with a ferocity that made her whole body spasm. She gasped for air as the waves of ecstasy slashed into her body with unforgiving intensity.

He pulled away from her mouth and rammed into her once, twice more, riding the orgasm with her until he exploded, ripples of breathless pleasure cutting through both of their bodies.

"Ah, Belle, damn it…" he rasped, deep and raw. He spurted into her for what seemed like minutes. Thick, hot, pulsing. And also open and vulnerable, giving himself to her, to the pleasure they shared.

His body collapsed on top of her, crushing her into the bed. She was still breathing heavy when he finally rolled off her, already calm and in control again. He didn't go far, pulling her into his arms, legs entangled and heat oozing from his body and into hers.

Her lids were heavy, satisfaction making her body feel lavish and lingering.

"Is it always like this with humans? For you?"

71

His body tensed and the beating of his heart against her ear got just a little louder, more insistent.

"It's never been like this, Belle," he whispered, tightening his arms around her. "It's never been so… intense, so dark."

Her heart fluttered. *Darkness*. So he felt it too. All-encompassing, so powerful it scared her. And still, too exquisite to ignore. Too beckoning.

She helplessly searched for something to say back, drawing a blank. Because she was finding it impossible not to agree with him.

When he pulled her closer, melting her into his body, she was glad to be distracted.

"What do you think of the compound?" he whispered and the sound resonated against her ear, sending shivers through her body.

She guessed what he was really asking was, *Is it so bad here?* And the truth was that it wasn't. She could somewhat understand the attraction of living in the compound. Food, safety, protection. And at least for her, pleasure. But in the end, she was still a prisoner. Nothing but slaves, her brother used to say. They were kept alive because they served a purpose.

"It's a nice prison, I guess," she answered.

Marcus' eyes darkened just a notch. She expected him to say something but instead he slid his hand towards her naked chest, making her gasp.

He smiled and her heart skipped a beat. It was the first time she'd seen a full smile on his face and she liked it. It was a wicked smile, the kind that said, *I've got this power and I know it*. It was also a glimpse into his vulnerable side, his human side. The side that made it easier to forget what he really was.

"I've never had an uncharmed human respond this way to my touch before. Something tells me you like it."

She did.

"Maybe I'm faking it," she taunted him.

Marcus' hand slid higher, until it was resting on her left breast, almost touching her nipple but not quite. The breath caught in her throat and her heart sped up, heat searing through her before she even realized what was happening.

Damn her body.

"I don't think so." He lowered his head to whisper the words against her lips.

She hated that he was right about this. She hated even more that he was nothing like she had expected the king to be. He was smart, passionate and a hell of a lot sexier than a vampire should be.

And her mind and heart were in a raging battle.

Kill him.

Love him.

Enslaver.

Lover.

Her biggest fear was that the longer she spent in his arms, the easier it would be for her heart to win the battle. And that wasn't something she could allow. That would be the ultimate betrayal—of her brother, of the people she had left behind. It would be betraying herself, even though part of her felt she was already doing that.

Marcus' lips closed over hers, awakening her body again, fueling the betrayal that flowed through her veins. He gripped her tightly, ravishing sounds escaping from her throat or his or both in a confusion of pleasure and need. As she closed her eyes and pushed against him, nails digging into his back, all she could think about was how exquisite he felt.

And, God help her, just how much she wanted to keep feeling him.

~*~

Belle felt pulsing and soft in his arms. It was the life pulse that only humans could provide—and that he suddenly couldn't get enough of. He swore internally. Every second he spent with Belle only served to increase his cravings. Not only for her blood, but also for her energy and how she made him feel.

"Belle, do you remember what I asked you about yesterday?"

Her body tensed up and he instinctively tightened his arms around her.

"The wild vampires?"

"Rabids," he corrected her. "That's what we call them."

She swallowed hard and he heard her heart thump just a little faster. He hated talking to her about this, but there was no avoiding it. He needed to know if she had any information that could help him—but more importantly, he needed to protect her. The only way to do that was to tell her the truth.

"What are they?" she finally asked and the words came out just slightly shaky.

He sighed. Nothing about this was easy. He got up and grabbed a robe, handing Belle another one. Her eyes followed him through the room before she put the robe on and got out from under the blankets, sitting on the edge of the bed.

"They're sick. Starving would be a better word, I guess."

Belle was quiet for a second, and he realized she was trying to process the information. She moved slowly and he wondered if he had taken too much blood. It wasn't a question he worried about often, but with Belle, keeping things under control was a lot more difficult than he had expected.

"So they're dying?" she finally asked.

"In a way. The difference is that starvation can take a long time to kill us." He could guess what the next question was going to be. "Years," he added before she could ask.

The silence in the room bothered him. He wanted to know what she was thinking, what she was feeling. He desperately wanted to charm her so he could ask whatever he wanted and get the truth out of her. Because that was what charming really was—a sort of truth serum, a surrendering of the mind.

"Why?" she finally asked. It was a basic, simple question, but he understood what she was really asking.

"Just as humans do, we require a minimum amount of nourishment to stay alive. If we don't get it, our organs start to shut down." He searched for the right words. "And our minds shut down along with our bodies."

"You… they go crazy?" The words came out warily.

"Yes. We call it 'the void' because everything becomes hollowed, as if you're slowly being swallowed by the darkness."

Belle shuddered.

"The less they eat, the faster the void spreads," he continued. "Until they can no longer think and they're just like rabid animals, destroying everything in their path, human or not."

He could almost hear the rush of thoughts flowing through her mind.

"So they're a danger to you too?"

"They'll attack anything, yes."

He paused for a second to let her absorb the meaning of those words.

"The compound?" she finally whispered.

He gave a quick nod. "We found some rabids nearby. Just a couple of hours away."

He stepped closer and studied her, savoring the warmth flowing from her.

"I want you to stay away from the outer walls, Belle. We have extra guards posted, but there's always a chance a rabid might get in."

He could smell her blood, rushing fast through her. It was a lot to grasp and process, but she seemed to be doing all right with the information. There was no panic in her eyes and although her heart was drumming at a frantic speed, everything else in her body was maintaining a steady pace: her breathing, her movements. It was certainly a lot more than he could have expected of any human—and he was impressed.

"How many are there?"

"Rabids? I don't know. Not that many right now, but the void spreads fast." He straightened and then ran a hand through his hair. "Eventually, humans won't be able to make it to the compound anymore because they'll get attacked on the roads."

Belle adjusted her position on the bed, crossing her legs. "Humans can still travel during daytime."

He could feel his own expression darken and wondered how much Belle could see in it. There were a lot of secrets in the vampire world, and he wasn't sure how many of those he wanted to give away.

"Not exactly," he finally said and his body got tense.

"What do you mean, not exactly? The rabids can't walk in daylight, can they?"

He took a step closer, his eyes locked on hers the whole time.

"We all can, Belle."

~*~

It couldn't be. For the past five years, her whole world had operated on the notion that vampires were night creatures.

They were the boogieman that came out to get you when the lights went out.

"That's not possible," she finally said, and the words came out as a whisper.

"The sun is debilitating, but it won't kill us right away," he explained. "Most of us avoid it because it takes time to get our energy back after being outside in daylight."

Her chest felt tight and the words danced in her head in a sort of dizzying haze that threatened to take over.

"You can... you can walk in daylight?"

Daylight was all she had. All that humanity had. All this time she had thought they were safe and it had all been a lie. The realization hit her hard. That meant vampire patrols could be out during the daytime, waiting in the shadows to hunt unsuspecting humans.

It also meant that the vampire back in the factory could have stepped into the light and grabbed her. The truth sent shivers down her spine.

He shook his head. "We rarely do because it's not exactly comfortable. It's almost... painful. But the rabids don't care. They lack the basic understanding to stay away from the sun."

She tried to process what Marcus was saying and it suddenly clicked. The rabids would hunt during the day too. They would be out in the prowl for food during the day and during the night. Humans would never be safe again, free to scavenge for supplies. If they didn't die on the roads, attacked by the vampires, they would die of starvation because they wouldn't be able to leave their hiding places. Why hadn't she ever heard rumors about vampires walking in daylight?

"How long can they stay out in the sun at once?"

There was an air of darkness around him. The kind that lingered in the air when somebody was revealing a sinister secret they'd been hoping to keep hidden. He didn't look

77

pleased about the confession, and Isabelle had to wonder why he was telling her at all.

"A few hours without any permanent damage," he finally said. "After that, deeper burns and maybe some scars, but I'm guessing they'll seek cover by then."

Words were buzzing in her head. There was another war raging in the world. One she didn't know anything about—and it could potentially be a lot worse than the one they'd already been through. If the void spread, if it reached every corner of the country, there would be no fighting to be had. No hope for a future in which humans could reclaim Earth as theirs. The rabids wouldn't have compounds and surrendering spots. They would be out hunting at all times, killing everything they ran into.

She was beginning to realize that maybe she had stumbled onto something a lot more important than killing the king of the vampires. She had found a secret that could destroy what little was left of her world. Despite her mounting fear, she couldn't help but wonder whether this discovery would change everything.

Perhaps more disturbing of all: she was relieved she had an excuse not to kill the king just yet.

CHAPTER 10

Marcus walked away from the bed and towards the window. The night was quiet, even to his ears. The wind whistled up and down the corridors and a few familiar voices drifted toward him. The harsh white lights above the walls gave the whole compound a ghostly luster. Right now, the place looked more like a prison than a castle. He couldn't see what was beyond the compound. Not from his window, anyway, as the walls were taller than any building inside. He could guess what was waiting beyond the barricade, though. Pitch black, deep darkness.

When the world had been alive, before the invasion, the darkness had always been a pulsing thing, alive with the breathing and the buzzing of people, animals and machines. Now, it was just a blanket of silence.

He didn't know why he'd told her about the rabids. Miles was right that he needed to be more careful, but there was something about her that stirred long-asleep emotions in him. Or maybe the answer was that he wasn't worried. After all, he was a hundred times stronger—and older—than she was. It was very unlikely that a frail human could do any real damage to any vampire, especially in vampire territory.

Even more telling, though, was the fact that her safety had suddenly become more important than keeping secrets. He did have a good reason for that, because the truth was that he could do damage control on a few humans knowing about their ability to walk in daylight if he had to—but if she got attacked by a rabid because she wasn't expecting to see one under the sun... well, he could never forgive himself for that.

His intention had been to find out more about her. The human who couldn't be charmed. He had even sent a convoy out to see if they could trace her way to the compound and figure out where she came from—and what secrets she had brought along with her. But the guards had run into a rabid just hours outside of the compound, and the mission objective had changed in seconds.

His main concern right now was to keep the rabids away. And to make sure his scientists managed to come up with a blood substitute as soon as possible. The void was curable, at least in theory. He wasn't sure where the dividing line was, however, as the last time the void had spread, everybody—including him—not infected had wasted no time and just ran away. His theory (and the scientists agreed) was that if you caught the void early enough, you could feed a rabid enough blood to revert the effects until he returned to normal. "Early enough" was tricky, though, because nobody knew exactly what that meant.

He did know that the blood supply was getting lower and lower. Nobody in the compound was going hungry because humans were still making it there. But the more rabids were out there, the fewer the chances that humans could get cross-country and into the compound before being attacked. And he was worried that at some point, his major problem wouldn't be how to keep things out—because the void would slip right into the compound.

He turned around to look at Belle, who seemed lost in thought. She looked so vulnerable sitting on his massive bed, so fragile—but he knew better. She had survived on the roads for at least a night. Hell, she had survived the invasion and the years after it, when food became scarce and illness was rampant.

Whatever fragile creature she appeared to be, he doubted it was the real her.

~*~

The first scream didn't sound like a human scream at all. In fact, it sounded like metal screeching, and Belle's first thought was that somebody was opening the entrance gate. People coming in? Darkness was still blanketing the surroundings, so it would have been risky trying to reach the compound.

Then she heard the sound again and realized it was a human voice. The terrified shriek of somebody who was staring death in the face.

Her eyes flew to Marcus, who was already dressed and heading for the door.

"Do *not* leave this room," he ordered and then disappeared in a blur of speed before she had a chance to say anything.

Another scream, but this time coming from somebody else. She grabbed her clothes and put them on in a rush, then ran to the window. Figures ran inhumanly fast towards the gate that separated her courtyard from the next one. Whatever was happening, it wasn't around her building. Flashes of grey eyes glimmered in the night, and she realized there were more vampires in the compound than she had first thought. Now that something was happening—whatever it was—they were all rushing out to take care of it.

A crack behind her made her jump. She turned around and found Miles standing near the bed. She hadn't heard the door open but there he was, almost as if he'd materialized inside the room.

She blinked. "What's going on?"

Miles didn't move, didn't flex a muscle. He was watching her intently, carefully, standing tall in his post. He was there as a guard. Either to protect her or to shield her from knowing what was going on outside. Either way, she didn't like it.

Another scream pierced the night, this time a shriek of agony that she knew wasn't human. It was a maddening sound that seemed to go on forever into the night. Behind it, a deep roar exploded. The hunter and the prey. Except that this time she wasn't sure who was hunting whom. The hairs on her arms stood up in response and panic engulfed her. She shivered and backed away from the window and towards the bed.

Miles must have sensed her fear because he moved closer. "It's OK. They can't get in here."

They. She was suddenly very aware of her fragility as a human. Her thoughts flew back to the house and to her brother. *Please be careful*, she thought. She knew very well none of them looked over their shoulders when out during the day. They were loud, they were careless, they moved about without paying attention to the shadows around them.

And then, all of a sudden, the compound was silent. So quiet, in fact, that she could hear her own ragged breath in the bleary air flowing into the room. Whatever had just happened was over and the silence following it was just as eerie as the sounds before had been.

She turned around to face Miles, eager for an explanation.

"Marcus will explain," was all he could offer.

The minutes that followed were overwhelmingly quiet. The shrieking was alive and whistling in her ears, which made the silence around her so much more glaring. She half-expected the sound to resume at any minute, but nothing happened. She was starting to back down towards the window when the door opened and Marcus appeared. His massive size filled the frame perfectly.

His eyes looked for hers and she sensed the subtle change in the air of the room. Then she noticed the blood on his clothes and her heart skipped a beat. Her body started moving before her thoughts finished forming and she lunged forward, reaching for him.

Then it clicked what she was doing and she stopped midway. "The blood?"

Marcus looked at her closely, words hanging in between them.

"Somebody got injured," he finally responded, and there was a darkness to his voice she hadn't heard before.

Her mind was reeling with questions. *Who? Why? What?* She looked at both vampires standing right in front of her, trying to figure out what side they were on. What side she was on.

And then the words were out before she could stop them. "I can help, I'm a doctor."

It wasn't necessarily a dangerous secret to spill, but her original intention had been to remain neutral. *Don't get involved, don't care about anybody.* The more she got involved, the more real the place would become—and she didn't want to have to worry about anybody when the time came to make a dangerous move.

Marcus was still, his gaze frozen on her. There were questions in his eyes, but they never made it into words. Instead, he turned around towards Miles.

"Go check with the guards. Find out where the breach happened."

When he returned his attention to her, there was a spark of something different in his eyes. Something that looked like… concern? She shook the idea off before it took hold.

"Stay close to me at all times," he ordered her, and she nodded.

For once she was glad to be surrounded by vampires.

Marcus whispered something to Miles and he disappeared again into the night.

The compound was quiet but she didn't have much time to contemplate the quietness, because Marcus was already marching towards the door. A chill ran down her spine and she swallowed hard.

"Stay close," Marcus repeated when they stepped out into the courtyard.

She hadn't paid much attention to the sounds of the compound the night before because she'd been in Marcus' arms. It was hard to take notice of the world around when his hands were on her and her skin was on fire. However, she was almost sure the compound had never been this quiet. Even during the day, when most—humans and vampires—slept, you could still hear the buzzing of words and fabric moving around in the corridors. But there was nothing like that going on at the moment. Silver eyes were everywhere, but vampires moved about in whispering sounds. Unless you were expecting them to be there, you would never hear them. Humans, on the other hand, were scarce. In fact, she didn't see a single person until they stepped into a smaller courtyard she had somewhat missed when surveying the compound.

There, the scene was very different. There was a small body lying on the ground. An older woman was sobbing while another figure hovered nearby. Neither person seemed to be panicking, and that made the whole scene much more difficult to absorb. Isabelle's mind flew back to the beginning of the invasion, when she'd lost people she loved. She remembered the panic, the desperation, the pain raging inside. The fact that these people weren't feeling that was a clear sign of how things had changed. The loss of human life was no longer a major tragedy. It was something people had come to accept as inevitable, as something you witnessed daily.

She rushed to the group, startling them in the process. The second figure, a frail-looking teen girl, stumbled back in surprise when she noticed the king standing there.

"It's OK," Isabelle whispered without looking up.

The body on the ground was a teenager. Her blonde hair was covered in blood and her clothes were half torn. She had major battle wounds, as well as lots of cuts and scrapes, probably from trying to fight her attacker. Belle suspected it hadn't done much good, as there was blood everywhere. In fact, she couldn't even find the source of the bleeding, because the girl was covered in blood.

She looked up towards the two people standing there.

"What's her name?"

"Lori," the older woman whispered.

Belle looked down, trying to get the girl's attention.

"Lori, can you hear me? Lori?"

But Lori was in shock, her gaze frozen into the night.

She looked up towards Marcus. "We need to get her somewhere inside, so I can check her wounds."

Before she could say anything else, Marcus picked the girl up without effort. He winced, and she wondered how much the smell and sight of blood was affecting him.

The teen girl, on the other hand, was panicking, her eyes frozen on Marcus. "Don't take her, don't take her."

Isabelle reached forward and grabbed the girl's hands. "I'm a doctor, I'll do what I can."

And although it wasn't exactly a lie, she wondered just how much she could do. Marcus was standing right by her side, loyal to the idea of not letting her out of his sight. She was wasting time trying to console these people, so she let go of the girl's hands and turned to the king. There was an aura of power around him. He seemed bigger than usual, towering over all of them. At that very moment, there was nobody else she would rather have standing right beside her. And the realization was both incredibly powerful and scary.

He nodded and started marching towards her building. His steps were effortless, as if the wounded girl weighed nothing in his arms. Belle wasn't sure where they were going, but Marcus had an obvious destination in mind. When he got within feet of her bedroom door, he quickly turned left, confusing her for a second.

And then he pushed the wall and a panel slid open. Belle's heart skipped a beat. *More secrets*, she thought. So that was how they were all able to move around and turn up in different places unexpectedly. Suddenly all the extra space in the long, empty corridors made sense.

She had been looking for answers in all the wrong places.

The passageway behind the door was narrow and dark. Claustrophobic was an even better word for it. At any other time, she would have had trouble breathing because of the walls closing in on her. Right now, she could barely keep up with Marcus, so she had no chance to think about anything but trying not to trip in the dark and fall flat on her face.

The corridor went on forever, and while she couldn't exactly tell, it seemed like the floor was slanted downhill. Underground. She was going underground.

"Marcus?"

"We're almost there," he answered from a few feet in front of her and she picked up the pace.

She was about to ask how much longer when she heard a soft click and then bright lights blinded her. She hurried into the new room and waited for a few seconds for her eyes to adjust to the brightness. A soft metallic tang hung in the air, mixing with the smell of… antiseptic?

As the blurriness slip away, the first thing she saw was the gurney in the middle of the room. Her gaze swiveled around, stopping for brief seconds on the metal instruments and the oxygen tanks. Where the hell was she?

Marcus placed the girl on the metal table and drew back a couple of steps. She reached for the girl's neck, searching for a sign of life.

"She's still alive," Marcus said.

"I can't find her pulse." She frantically probed with her fingers on the girl's cold skin.

"It's there, I can hear it."

She searched for scissors in nearby drawers and started cutting the girl's clothes as soon as she found a pair. She could hear her own heavy breathing in the quietness of the room. It was such an alien sound, it made her uneasy. To her, emergency rooms had a heavy buzzing to them—doors sliding, the squeaking and beeping of machines coming to life, the rattle of metal instruments hitting the trays. Here, it was just her. Lori was too far gone to make any sounds, and Marcus was breathing softly, no other sounds coming out of him as he observed her work around the table.

"Can you tell where the blood is coming from?" she asked him.

"Abdomen," he responded, and she could hear the heaviness in his voice again.

The thick smell of blood permeated the room.

She reached around for rubber gloves and slapped them on, then slid her fingers over the girl's pulsating stomach. There. A gash at least five inches long. Maybe more. She cleared the blood as best as she could, then examined the opening. It didn't seem deep enough to have reached any organs, but without the proper equipment, it was impossible to tell.

Lori's breath was slowing down. She was slipping through Belle's fingers and there was nothing she could do about it.

~*~

Marcus couldn't keep his eyes off her. He had been hoping for a glimpse of the real Isabelle, the one she had been before coming to the compound—and this was a bright flash into her world. Truth was, he was a lot more interested in what she was doing than in the girl on the gurney. Probably because the girl on the gurney wasn't going to make it.

The smell of blood held many clues. It could tell you when somebody was sick or full of life. It could give you clues into a person's past and future.

In the case of the girl in the room, the smell said death was close.

Maybe a massive blood transfusion would save her. Maybe. But blood was in short supply and he wasn't about to share what little they had. He didn't know the girl well, but that wasn't the reason why. In the end, his loyalty lay with the ones like him. He had a slightly better opinion of humans than

Patrick did, but when it came time to make a choice, there were no questions as to where his loyalties were.

Death took a step closer.

Belle was still frantically trying to work a miracle, but the flow of blood was constant. It was also slowing down. Not because what she was doing was helping, but because the girl was running out of blood.

Marcus shook his head. "Let her go, Belle. There's nothing else you can do."

"No." The certainty in her voice was in part conviction and in part challenge. She was telling him to stay out of it, to let her make her own decisions. But Marcus knew it was all just a waste of time and he just wanted to get her away from there.

He wasn't used to women—or to anybody, for that matter—telling him "no." And right now, with all the chaos of the attack, it was the last thing he wanted to deal with. He had to get back to Miles and figure out exactly what had happened. He also needed to get her into a secure area so he could go out to attend to his business without having to worry about her.

He stepped forward and grabbed her arm. "Belle, let her go."

"No!"

She tried to jerk her arm free, but Marcus anticipated her move and held on to her tight, dragging her towards him and away from the table.

"She'll be dead in a minute," he told her and that seemed to work, because Belle stopped resisting and eased back against his chest.

He wrapped his arms around her and felt the soft tremor running through her body. He half-expected Belle to start crying, but the slight shivering was the only indication of how she was feeling.

He remained still, holding on to her and feeling the warmth of her body slipping into his. She fit perfectly against his body, every curve sliding into the right place and producing the right amount of electricity. Her body was struggling to remain still and it was obvious she was making a tremendous effort not to show any emotions.

Without letting go, he leaned his head forward, moving his lips towards her ear. Even now, her smell was intoxicating, the softness of her essence sending an electric pulse down his body.

"It's OK, Belle. You don't have to be brave."

Her body tensed for a second, then relaxed back into his arms.

"I want to get out of here."

He let her go so she could turn around to face him. "I'll get somebody to take care of this."

She swallowed hard and took a step backwards. "How?"

"We have to burn the bodies," he explained. "Burying them would attract the rabids. They can track smells underground."

Her whole face contracted in a gesture of revulsion, but she said nothing. Instead, she looked at the girl one more time, frozen forever in a gesture of pain and desperation. She extended a hand forward, as if she was planning on checking for a pulse one more time, but the movement stopped before she reached the bloody skin. "I want to get out of here, Marcus."

He didn't have to be told again. "Let's go."

Before she had time to think, he grabbed her hand and walked towards the tunnels. She flinched for a second but made no effort to get free. Instead, she moved closer to his body as they approached the darkness of the underground.

And Marcus found himself thinking that he actually relished the protector role much more than he had expected.

CHAPTER 11

The idea first crossed his mind the second he had seen her working on the girl on the gurney. Now that she was back in her room and he had a chance to think things through, the idea was back and stronger than ever.

Not that he needed to explain his decisions to anybody, but Miles wouldn't be happy to hear what he was thinking.

Because he was seriously considering bringing Belle into the lab.

He had a lot of great scientific minds working in the lab, but none of them was a trained physician. In fact, none of them was truly an expert in the human body.

Up until this very moment, there had never been any alliances between vampires and humans—and with good reason. The more humans knew about vampires, the more chances they had to fight against them. A few centuries ago, he wouldn't have even considered letting a human into his secrets.

But these were different times. Desperate times. And letting a human work alongside his scientists could be the only hope both species had for survival.

He grabbed the back of his neck and sighed. He could feel things slipping out of control a little bit more every day. If he didn't find an answer soon, everybody would be in trouble.

He groaned and sat back against his chair.

This was far from his dream of a vampire-run world. It was a lot closer to his idea of a nightmare.

A soft knock on the door brought him back to reality.

"Come in."

Miles had two guards with him when he stepped into the room. They looked somber and Marcus could smell the blood on his clothes. Vampire blood.

"What happened?"

Jaco took a step closer. "Two rabids got into the compound."

Marcus stood still, absorbing the news.

"How?"

The guards wavered slightly under his gaze.

"We don't know, My Lord. We have guards on every corner. And the rabids are not exactly the quietest, but we still didn't hear them getting in."

Marcus turned to Miles for an answer.

"I don't know what to say," Miles answered. "Jaco's right. We have no idea how they got in. Unless…"

"Unless they got in through the tunnels somehow," Jaco interrupted.

Marcus' expression hardened. "How could they get in through the tunnels? There are only two exits to the outside through the tunnels and they can only be opened from the inside."

Then he paused and studied Miles' face for a second. "Are you saying somebody let them in?"

"I don't know," Miles said. "Maybe."

Jaco shook his head. "And if that's the case, we have bigger problems ahead, because we found two more rabids right outside the compound, near the east wall."

"They put up quite a fight," Miles added. "And we lost two humans in the chaos. Shredded to pieces in seconds."

"Three humans," Marcus corrected, remembering the girl on the gurney.

Miles studied him with interest, but said nothing. "We managed to kill all the rabids we found, but unless we figure out how they got in, I don't think this will be the last time we have to deal with them."

"They're getting desperate, My Lord," Jaco added. "And the hungrier they get, the bolder they'll get too."

Marcus knew it. It could only get worse from then on unless something changed. It was time to stop waiting and start moving.

"Miles, put a search party together and send them out. Make that two groups, actually, and send them in opposite directions. Canvas the surroundings and search for hiding places. They're hiding somewhere, so let's find out where before they decide to attack again."

Miles nodded. "I can take a search party up north..."

"No," Marcus interrupted. "I need you here. I want to spend some time figuring out the safety of the tunnels and the walls. Jaco can take one of the groups, and find somebody to lead the second one."

Miles groaned softly but said nothing.

"Grayson would do," Jaco said.

Miles nodded. "I agree."

Marcus got up and walked towards the window. The compound was quieter than usual. He figured all the humans were hiding, trying to cope with the events.

"What's the nearest town?" Marcus asked without turning around to face the guards.

"Franklin, I think," Miles said. "About four hours away, but it's been abandoned for years."

"Even more reason to search it, then. The rabids who are still somewhat lucid should be looking for safer sleeping places, so search in dark basements and attics. The sicker ones might be less careful, so look in houses. They'll be following any remaining human smell they can catch. Look in schools and hospitals too."

Miles looked at Jaco and a silent acknowledgement passed between them.

"Drive, don't walk," Marcus added. "I don't want you to take any unnecessary risks."

Miles groaned. "Cars will just slow the groups down."

"They will also serve as shields. I don't want the groups to get to town only to discover there's a hundred rabids there. Park near the edge of town if you're worried about noise. And if things get tough, get out. We're not looking for war right now. We're not ready."

"Kill only if we have to?"

"Kill if you can," Marcus corrected. "But not at the risk of anybody in the group. I'm more concerned with finding out what we're up against."

He turned around and backed away from the window.

"Send the groups out and then come back here," he told Miles. "We're going to go on a little exploring trip inside the tunnels. I'm ready to make somebody pay for this."

Miles gave a short nod. "All I need is thirty minutes to get things ready."

"Go," Marcus said. "I'll be ready when you get back here."

The guards turned around and marched right out of the room.

The truth was that he was glad for the little time alone to get his thoughts in order. *Belle.* Even now, the memory of her skin, feverish under his touch, kept looping through his mind. What he really wanted was to head over to her bedroom and get into bed with her. Hold her, fuck her, drink from her. Over and over again.

He'd thought that once she was his, the hunger would recede. Instead, it was getting stronger. Her blood was intoxicating, but so was her taste and the smell of her body reacting to his. His body tightened at the memories of what had happened just hours before. Then his thoughts trailed off to his teeth sinking into her inner thigh, the silky blood flowing into his mouth.

He groaned and walked back towards the window. The predator in him was awakening and he had to fight to push it down. *Not now.* The pleasures of the flesh would have to wait, because he had other things to tend to.

Other pleasures.

Like finding the one responsible for tonight's attack.

In fact, he was looking forward to peeling the skin off the traitor before he bled him to death. Human or vampire, it didn't matter. He was hungry for blood and ready to kill.

CHAPTER 12

As she wrapped herself in a towel, Belle turned around and looked at the bathtub. *Blood water*, she thought. Then she immediately pulled the stopper to let the water stream out.

It had been a long time since she'd played savior and failed. Sure, she had lost patients in the ER, but the loss there had felt much different. Not because those lives had been any less precious to her, but because here, in the aftermath of destruction, each human life lost was a different kind of tragedy. Every time a human died, they were all a step closer to extinction.

Funny that after centuries of destroying the oceans and polluting the Earth, humans were going to disappear before many of the other creatures on the planet. In fact, she suspected many animals were now thriving, thanks to the low number of hunters walking around.

She stepped out of the bathroom and into the bedroom, looking for some clean clothes in her ridiculously well-stocked wardrobe.

When the invasion had first begun, she—and everybody she knew—had fantasized about escaping to far-away lands. They had even concocted plans of setting off towards some deserted island somewhere, where the chances of running into a vampire would be lower. That was back then, when the monsters were focused on attacking the cities. It didn't take long before the roads became just as dangerous and they had no choice but to hide.

They had lost TV and internet signals before it was clear what was going on around the world. So she lied to herself, even though a little voice inside told her there was no safe place left anywhere, no utopian land where people still reigned.

So yes, every human life lost was a tragedy, now more than ever.

She slipped into a soft pink shirt and a pair of jeans, then lay back on the bed. She wanted to go out, to search for the two women she'd seen with Lori. But there was a guard right outside her door. She knew because she'd already tried to get out—and had been told, in just a few words, that she wouldn't be going anywhere unless Marcus authorized it.

Marcus. She hated that she now thought of him as an individual with a name. He was no longer "the king of the monsters" or "a vampire." He was Marcus. Marcus who could make her feel the most exquisite of pleasures. Marcus who would go out into the compound to pick up a dying girl and then lead her into a secret room. Marcus who held her while she was breaking down and whispered sweet words in her ear.

Where was the monster? Why wasn't he there? He appeared too composed, too sane, too... human. And it was scaring her more than she ever thought possible.

Don't think of him as human, she reminded herself.

But deep down, she knew it was too late. He was already Marcus.

If she was going to kill him, it had to be soon, because she could feel her resolution wavering, breaking down by the minute. By the second.

Part of her wished he would do something heartless, let the monster come out. Give her a reason to plunge a knife—*one you don't have*, she reminded herself—into his heart.

Her stomach tightened at the thought of hurting him. She cursed and stood up with a heavy sigh. If she could at least get out of the room, she could try to figure out the compound better. She had a feeling that the secret door they had gone through wasn't the only one. Hadn't Miles materialized into her room a couple of times? And on the first morning, she'd found a fire crackling and her clothes gone.

She walked towards one of the walls, looking for anything that could trigger a locking hidden mechanism. If there was a concealed door there, she would find it. After all, she had all the time in the world.

‿*‿

The darkness of the tunnels loomed in front of Marcus for what seemed like miles. To humans, the labyrinth of cavern-like tunnels would be impossible to maneuver, but not only could he see in the darkness of the underground, both Miles and he knew the tunnels extremely well. If he wanted, he could run to the other end with his eyes closed.

Tonight, though, they were both stepping lightly. If there was somebody—or something—hiding in the shadows, Marcus wanted to make sure they'd surprise him.

They turned around a corner and Miles pointed out something in the distance. A sliver of light. Impossible for human eyes to detect but very clear to them. Marcus nodded in response and then crouched in the darkness, waiting for the slight creak of something moving in the tunnels.

Five seconds. Ten. The tunnels were dead quiet. He glanced at Miles and saw him nod. Then both of them got up and kept moving forward. They stopped along the way a few times to search for whispers in the dark, but there was nothing there. After the third or fourth time, he was convinced they were alone down there. And if that was the case, the light back at the end of the tunnel was nothing but the moonlight, streaming through a scrape in the door.

The musty odor of the tunnel was slightly milder tonight. He narrowed his hearing to concentrate on the direction of the door. The world outside the compound was quiet—at least for now.

He turned around to face Miles, who was right behind him. "What do you think?"

"Everything looks normal."

"I smell vampire blood."

Miles nodded. "There were guards patrolling down here less than an hour ago."

"Let's go check the other tunnel, then."

The second tunnel was just as quiet as the first one. If rabids had gone through it, their smell was long gone, diluted by the steps of the vampires that came right after them. And one thing was certain: there was no warm human smell down in the darkness. If somebody had opened the door to let the rabids in, it had been one of his own.

"Fuck," Marcus said as they stepped back into the courtyard.

Miles was back to his usual quiet self, his eyes prodding into the surrounding darkness for anything unusual. "I'll send some guards to watch the doors."

Marcus moved away from the wall and into the inviting softness of the night. Belle's light was off but the moonlight glided into her room, giving him a peek into the darkness. "Who do we really trust?" he finally asked.

Miles hesitated for a second longer than he would have liked. Marcus knew what that meant: his friend was also having doubts about the loyalty of the vampires in the compound.

"I have a few names in mind," he said. "Do you want a list?"

Marcus shook his head. "No, if there's anybody I trust, it's you. Just get somebody there tonight."

Then he looked up again and saw the curtains in Belle's room flicker for a second. He wanted to go up and check on her. No, that wasn't true. He wanted to feed on her, slip into her, savor her. But he knew that if he stepped into the room, he wouldn't be able to leave for hours.

He looked at Miles. "And keep the guard outside her door."

"She can't be charmed, can she?"

Marcus' gaze narrowed. "Who else has noticed it?"

"Nobody, as far as I can tell. Not yet anyway." Then, after a brief moment of hesitation, "How did you get her into bed without charming her?"

Marcus remembered her thundering heart as he got closer. "Oh, she came very willingly."

Miles watched him with obvious interest and Marcus could see the traces of a smile forming on the usually stone face. "I guess I understand now."

"Understand what?"

"Why you've suddenly decided you needed a pet after so many centuries," Miles said.

Marcus frowned and looked back up towards the window. "Let's just make sure we keep this between us for now. I wouldn't want my enemies knowing about it."

A second passed. Then another. Miles focused his eyes on the window, almost as if studying the wavering of the curtains in the wind. There was a heaviness in the air, the kind that came around when questions were left unanswered and secrets were hushed. "How much do you care about her?"

Marcus groaned and turned his gaze towards his friend. He had been avoiding that question for the past few days, worried that he would uncover something about himself that he'd prefer to keep buried. Because the truth was that vampires couldn't afford to feel anything for a human. They were too fragile, too volatile. They were the prey and he was the hunter.

He ran a hand through his hair before letting out a breath. "More than I'm ready to admit right now," he finally said. Miles straightened, his eyes still locked on the second floor window. "Then let's make sure it remains a secret."

Marcus nodded and looked up. The heaviness in the air seemed to slip into his chest. He was worried. Not only for her safety, but for the safety of everybody in the compound, human or not. Because if there was anything his enemies would love, it would be to find out the king had a weak spot.

When he finally spoke, his voice was tight. "Let's go check the walls, Miles. I could use the distraction."

_*_

After an hour of searching every inch of the walls in her room, Belle was still nowhere closer to finding a secret door. If there was one in her room, the mechanism was a lot more clever—and much better hidden—than she had first expected. She sighed in exasperation and walked towards the door. As soon as she touched the door handle, the vampire on the other side pushed the door ajar and eyed her steadily.

Did she know him? She didn't think so. Miles wasn't the friendliest of vampires, but at least he didn't look as menacing as the one on the other side of her door right now. The steely spark in his eyes was the closest to warmth in his whole expression; everything else was just stone. The idea of trying to reason with him briefly crossed her mind, but she waved it away. There was no way she was getting past the guard and she knew it.

She stepped back into the room and the door closed behind her. A storm was raging in her mind and trying to make sense of anything was proving harder and harder. Why was she being guarded? Suddenly her interests were splitting in an assortment of different directions. She wanted to go out and search for the two women she'd seen with Lori. She also wanted to find at least one of what she suspected were many secret doors in the compound—except that searching for them could leave her exposed. If there was a guard posted outside her door during the night, it made sense to think they were also keeping tabs on her during the day somehow. And by "they," she really meant Marcus.

Maybe all the little secrets he was letting out were finally weighing heavily in his mind and he had decided she needed to be watched. Except that she doubted that was the case. In fact, she was almost sure that the king wasn't the kind of man… the kind of creature… who would regret his decisions. If he had told her about the daylight immunity, he had to have a reason for it. Just because she wasn't aware of what that reason was didn't mean it didn't exist.

She paced around for a few seconds before heading towards the window above her bed. Dark clouds were gathering in the distance, bringing with them a faint rumble of thunder.

CHAPTER 13

She'd finally fallen asleep sometime in the middle of the night. Even then, her sleep was plagued with flashes of death, chaos and disaster. At one point in her dreams, she saw her brother, running away through the open fields near the house. He kept trying to tell her something, but she couldn't make out the words. His lips moved as he screamed, but the sound got lost into the echoing darkness. Even worse, she hadn't even tried to help him or move towards him. Instead, she'd just stood there, watching him run into the gloom of the night.

And then the rabids had come up crawling through the land, up from the belly of the underground. Their eyes were bloodshot and insane. One, two, ten. Suddenly there were dozens of them running after Shawn. But she still didn't move. She stood frozen in place, next to the king, watching as the rabids tore into her brother's body. The smell of death lingered in the air, thick and perfume-like. It was such a familiar odor, such a well-known thickness in the air, that it almost felt comforting. *Death is all you know*, something from inside her whispered.

And then she heard the screams, half beast and half human. Sounds of agony that tore through her skin and reverberated in her chest.

She woke up panting, her heart hammering so loud against her ribs that her entire chest hurt. Sitting on the bed, she buried her face in her hands and took a few deep breaths. *Calm down, damn it. It was just a dream.*

But she wasn't so sure it had been. After all, there was at least a small chance the house was in danger. A chance her brother had gone looking for her and run into the rabids. An immense sense of dread filled her chest and sent her heart into a frantic race. *It's OK, they're OK*, she told herself, even though she had trouble believing the words.

She looked towards the window and the rain tapping quietly against the glass. She had stopped using a watch a long time ago because time no longer mattered. There was nowhere to go, nowhere to be. Right now, though, she would've liked to know what time it was. Despite the storm outside, the sky was bright, probably closer to noon than to early morning. Still, her body felt tattered, like she had barely rested.

When she finally gathered enough strength to get up, she walked to the bathroom and placed her whole head under the tap. The cold water sent a shiver down her spine but also helped her wake up. It would be a while before she stopped loving the luxury of running water.

She rubbed her hair with a towel and then walked towards the door. Then she leaned against it, trying to detect any small sounds coming from the other side.

Nothing.

The logical deduction would've been that the guard was gone, since it was daylight, but she now knew better. He could easily be standing on the other side, holding his post. She eyed the windows, which were too small—and probably too high up—to use safely and then groaned in frustration.

She needed to get out of the room at some point during the day. Not only to search the compound and see if she could find any of the secret doors, but also because she wanted to find Lori's friends. She wasn't sure if they'd been told anything about her death. If they hadn't, they deserved to hear it from her, not from one of the vampires. Back at the hospital, she had always insisted on being the one delivering the news when she lost a patient, and today didn't have to be any different. Or at least she didn't *want* it to be different.

She was still leaning close to the door when somebody knocked. She jumped back in surprise, her heart pounding.

The second knock was just as soft, but this time it came with a whispering voice attached to it. "Isabelle?"

Vicki. She took a deep breath, then reached forward and opened the door. The guard was gone.

The woman's face was alit with surprise, as if she couldn't believe Isabelle was actually there. She remained motionless for a few seconds, looking over Belle's shoulder and into the room, then back to her face.

"It's true, then," she finally said, and there was a hint of accusation in her voice.

Isabelle frowned slightly. "I was heading to the kitchen, do you want to come along?"

"Can I see the room first?"

Isabelle looked over the woman's shoulder. "Have you seen any guards around?"

Vicki seemed to consider her words for a second, then scoffed. "What do you mean, guards? It's daytime."

So it was a secret after all, the immunity to daylight. Isabelle wondered if it was a wise thing keeping it a secret, considering the events of the night before.

She hesitated for a second, then stepped aside. "Come in."

She had no idea where the rest of the humans in the compound slept, but she could bet it wasn't in a room like hers. Suddenly, she felt guilty. Not because she had the best room and others didn't, but because she couldn't explain right now why it was a good thing that she had it. Now that she knew there were secret doors and passageways below the compound, she couldn't be sure who was watching and when. For all she knew, there was a vampire behind a peephole just a few feet away. There was no way she could risk speaking about her plans or opening up to anybody. Especially not in her room.

Vicki's eyes kept moving around the room, trying to take it all in. When she finally turned around to face Isabelle, her face was laced with tension and something else. Jealousy?

"So the rumors are true," she said. "You are the king's pet."

Belle groaned. "I hate that word, but I guess the answer is yes."

Vicki sat down on her bed and Isabelle had an immediate urge to actually push her out the door.

"What is he like?"

How was she supposed to answer a question like that? Not with the truth, definitely. Because telling Vicki the truth meant she had to admit it to herself first.

"I don't know." She shook her head, trying to find the right words to lie properly.

"I've been in the compound for four years and I've never seen him take a pet," Vicki said, and that spark of recrimination was back in her voice. "He's always so distant, so away from everything and everybody. We really don't know anything about him."

Isabelle shifted on her feet. "Please don't talk about us as if we're animals. Pet is their word, not ours."

Vicki shrugged, basically ignoring her words. "Being his does have some privileges," she said as she looked around the room one more time.

"I don't care about the room."

"Is he... violent?"

It sounded as if Vicki was hoping the answer was yes. Was this what it was all about? So much darkness around them and people were still worrying about who got the better house and the shinier car. Or, in this case, the fanciest room.

She didn't have the patience to deal with this stuff any longer. Or maybe she just didn't care anymore. The past twenty-four hours had been exhausting, she was in a bad mood and she hadn't done any of the things she wanted—needed— to do, including finding the door and searching for Lori's friends. Petty jealousy was the last thing she wanted to deal with at the moment.

"I need food," she answered, wanting to hurry Vicki up towards the door. "Let's just get out of here."

Vicki's gaze was fixed on hers but she was quiet. Even more obviously, she was annoyed. And all of a sudden, Belle was annoyed too. How long had Vicki said she'd been at the compound? At least four years. So she had jumped into the compound opportunity as soon as it became an option. And now she was wondering how come the newcomer had ended up with the shinier car. As if the whole thing had anything to do with seniority.

She pointed to the door again and made a motion for both of them to go. No way she was leaving this woman alone in her room. Vicki let out a sigh of frustration and then headed out without saying another word.

If it came time to fight and pick sides, Isabelle was pretty sure Vicki wasn't going to stand on her side. The shinier car side was apparently a lot more appealing.

CHAPTER 14

It had been a day of nothingness. She had spent most of the afternoon trying to find Lori's friends without luck. How in the world did somebody disappear within the walls of the compound? Unless they both happened to be walking constantly ahead of her without her knowing it.

On top of that, the encounter with Vicki nagged in the back of her mind. The whole conversation had left a bad taste in her mouth and a sort of heaviness in her stomach. Vicki had followed her to the kitchen, trying to continue a conversation she had no intentions of indulging. Only when Vicki realized she wasn't going to get any answers had she finally had left Isabelle alone. Even then, though, the ringing of poorly controlled jealousy had stayed with Isabelle throughout the rest of the day.

So much that even when she had managed to find what she thought was one of the secret doors—tucked away at the end of one of those going-nowhere corridors—she just couldn't get excited enough about it. Not that it would have made any difference, because finding the door didn't mean she could open it. There was some sort of hidden mechanism or code needed for the door to slide open—and she had no idea how to get it to happen.

So when Marcus had sent for her that evening, just as the sun was setting down, she'd been more than just glad to go to him. She hadn't even realized it until then, but she'd been looking forward to his company, to his voice undulating in the room and into her body and her blood like music. Looking forward to his touch that awoke every single cell in her body. It was as if her body was organically hungry for him, missing him, aching for his energy. She didn't like the feeling of urgency she was experiencing, but that didn't mean it was any less real.

The second she stepped into his room, however, the air was different. He turned to look at her and his whole expression was darker than usual. Still, at the sight of her, his body relaxed, the ripples of his muscles easing down as she moved closer. He still looked massive and no doubt intimidating to anybody else, but she was beginning to understand the subtleties of his movements. To learn when the king had things weighing on his mind.

All of a sudden, she felt an unbearable urge to hold him and that set alarms off in both her mind and her body. It was a visceral reaction to his discomfort and one she could neither control nor deny. She wanted to comfort him, take the worry away. Comfort the monster. Comfort *her* monster, her mind corrected, and her heart went into a race.

He noticed right away, his eyes moving to her chest to trace the source of the sound. Then they immediately softened and his breath changed cadence to match the beating of her heart.

"Can you keep a secret, Belle?"

She froze, her body suddenly on edge. A secret. *Another secret*. For a second, she wanted to say no. *Don't tell me your secrets, Marcus. I'm the enemy.* Then she remembered her brother and the people back at the house.

"Of course," she replied, hoping he wouldn't notice the slight wavering in her voice.

He hesitated for a fraction of a second. Just a slight flicker of apprehension while his eyes probed hers. Never had she been more glad she couldn't be charmed. What kind of information would he have been able to get out of her if she'd been under his spell? Everything? Then he headed towards the door, his perfect form filling the room as he walked away from her.

"Follow me."

And Belle had a fleeting thought: she was almost sure she'd follow him to the end of the world.

‐*‐

This time she stayed close to him as they walked down the tunnels. She still couldn't see anything and twice she tripped and ended up crashing against his massive back. The tunnels had obviously not been constructed with humans in mind, as they were pitch black. Darkness down there not only looked thick, it also smelled thick. She had the distinct feeling that if she stretched her arms to the sides, she would be able to actually touch the shadows.

There was also a sort of murmuring quality to the tunnels. At first she'd thought it was her ears playing tricks on her, but after a couple of minutes, she realized the sounds were real, even though she couldn't quite place them. It was like the tunnels were breathing all around her, whistling a tune of dense obscurity into her ears.

"Are we alone down here?"

Marcus continued walking in front of her and at first she thought maybe he was ignoring her question. The silence stretched out for seconds, as the whispering of the tunnels seemed to grow more intense.

"In a way," he finally responded.

What the hell does that mean, in a way? She sighed and then quickly turned around when she felt something moving in the distance. It disoriented her for a second and she lost track of which way was forward until he spoke again.

"What is it?" he asked.

She swallowed hard and the sound bounced off the walls and intensified before fading off, as if devoured by the darkness.

"I swear this place feels alive," she finally said, moving closer to him. "Are you sure nobody is watching?"

She could almost hear his smile forming. "I didn't say nobody's watching. They're just not watching from *right here*."

"What does that even mean, not from right here? Are there peepholes in the walls?" And as if it made sense, she actually extended her hand and touched the walls, searching for tiny holes. The walls felt dry and softly crumbled under her fingers. She moved her hand away with a cry of surprise.

"Relax, Belle. There are doors along the way, like the one to the room you used last night." He reached for her and grabbed her hand. "We're almost there."

The touch felt electric. So warm and *oh-so-right*. Screams started to rise from inside her, telling her to let go, to not enjoy his fingers interlacing with hers in a firm grip. But she closed her eyes for a second, trying to silence them. She could convince herself he was the enemy most of the time, but when they touched, the buzzing of electricity between them was impossible to ignore and it made his all-encompassing, powerful presence almost too real to handle.

It also made the darkness a lot more bearable.

_*_

Letting Belle into his secrets was becoming some sort of a routine. This time, at least, was to his benefit. Or at least he was hoping it would be.

Her hand wiggled softly in his and instinctively, he squeezed just a little harder. To him, the tunnels were peaceful. A cry away from the sounds of the night and the whispering of danger outside the walls. When he had them built, he'd specifically requested that they kept them as close as possible to their natural state—crumbling earth rather than perfectly smooth walls. It made the tunnels and the darkness feel welcoming—and he liked it.

Of course, he could also see in the dark, so maybe the tunnels didn't feel as welcoming for mortals walking blindly through them.

Belle's heart was thundering. It was a sound he spent hours listening to while she slept. Although vampires had a heartbeat, it was a very different kind. His heart beat softly, sleepily. The kind of sound you expected from somebody ancient and immune to disease or stress—which he certainly was. Belle's heart rate was very much different. It had a mind of its own, spiking up and softening down depending on her mood and—much to his satisfaction—also depending on how close he was to her.

Right now, her heart rate had been jumping up every time it caught a creak or a shred of movement. But the second his hand touched hers, it went into a race. Her blood sped up and the echoing of the thumps against her chest became all the more clear. It was such an enticing sound, it instantly awoke his hunger. It took a near unbearable effort to push the animal down and keep walking. For a second, he was too distracted to even answer back when she asked a question. Something about the whispering of the tunnels around them.

The smell of her blood blended in with the wildness of the earth around them. It was an exquisite mix and he wished he could turn around and take her right there. Every hunter cell in his body was fighting to take over and he found himself struggling to push them down.

When he saw the blackness ahead slowly melting into grey, he was just glad the walk was almost over.

"There." He pointed it out to her.

After a few more seconds, the corridors started to become lighter, as if a grey sunset was slowly moving in towards them. It took several more steps before they arrived to the small entry hall and stopped right in front of a metal door.

This was it. Once he opened the door and they stepped in, there was no turning back. *Too late to change your mind, Marcus*, he told himself, and pushed the door open.

˗*˗

Seeing the tunnels get lighter had prompted her to sigh in relief. Marcus seemed at ease in the tunnels, but to her, they were just frightening. Complete darkness was a scary place to be—you couldn't anticipate what was coming at you and from where. And after years of being afraid of the dark, being devoured by it was probably one of the most terrifying things she could think of. Her mind kept playing tricks on her, screaming for her to be afraid of the monsters hiding in the dark. It was almost easy to forget that she was holding the hand of the biggest monster of all—and feeling safe because of the warm electric charge surging between them.

She wasn't sure what to expect at the end of the tunnel, but it certainly wasn't the bluish metal door that was waiting for them. Maybe because all the other doors seemed to be so secrete, so I'm-here-but-I'm not, that this one seemed out of place—and somehow more frightening than all the other ones she couldn't see.

Marcus said nothing as he pushed the door open, and her whole body tensed up in expectation. She held her breath and got closer to him, using him as a shield.

The world on the other side of the door stopped as the king stepped in. The brightness of the room attacked her eyes without mercy. She blinked twice, then closed her eyes for a few seconds to fight the tears forming. *Breathe*, she told herself, *just breathe*. When she opened them again and was able to focus, she gasped.

She was looking at one of the most advanced laboratories she had ever seen outside of a hospital. The room from the night before was nothing compared to the giant space opening up before her.

Only after she had absorbed every little detail in the lab did she notice the vampires dressed in white coats and staring at her.

"My Lord, we weren't expecting you here," one of them said to the king, although his eyes were locked on Isabelle.

She was just as fascinated with the view in front of her as they seemed to be with her. Why did he have a medical setup under the compound? Obviously the room she'd used the other night had been just a tiny part of something much bigger. Something beyond her wildest expectations.

"Cyrus, this is Belle," Marcus said, cocking his head slightly to the side, towards her. As if there was any doubt of who or what she was.

The vampire drifted his whole body slightly forward, and the skin on her arms quivered in response. The vampires here had a different air about them, one she didn't quite like. The white coats didn't help, either. She felt like an intruder snooping into a secret testing facility.

She looked around, searching for test tubes and blood-testing machinery. Lancets, tourniquets, and test stripes were spread around the room, sitting on tables and neatly organized on the shelves. Machines hummed in the background: a lab centrifuge, electrosurgery generators, cryosurgical systems. All you needed if you were playing around with blood.

Her heart hammered faster in her chest. Was that what they were doing?

"Belle?"

Was he testing her? Trying to see how much she could figure out before he actually explained what the hell was going on?

Her mind was spinning when she turned around to look at him. "What kind of blood are you testing?"

Marcus' eyes flickered for a quick second. They got slightly darker, then back to light again. "Fake blood," he said.

She shook her head slightly, as if that could help make her mind clearer. "What do you mean, fake blood? You mean a blood substitute?"

The vampire in the white coat searched for the answer in the king's eyes. When Marcus nodded, he shook his head. "No, we're working on artificial blood."

It took a second for the information to click, but when it did, her heart skipped a beat. "Artificial blood?" Her mind was buzzing with questions and trying to pick which one to ask first was giving her a headache. "As in, to completely replace human blood?"

"That's right," the vampire confirmed.

It didn't make any sense. The compound was full of people and she didn't expect any of the vampires up there to be truly hungry. Unless he had something bigger in mind.

"Why?"

"We're trying to figure out the perfect combination of nutrients *for us*," the vampire—Cyrus?—answered. "So far, it hasn't quite worked. We're close, but something's missing."

Marcus shifted slightly next to her and his arm brushed hers. The electricity of the touch was enough to get her attention and make her turn towards him. He seemed different, as if the whole world had suddenly tipped on its axis and he had been staring at it while it was happening. There was a deep light coming through his eyes—not from, but through them, from somewhere deep inside—and the instant she focused on them, something hit her. She blinked, trying to absorb the emotions and the knowledge he was letting out. *Can you keep a secret, Belle?* he had said. Never in a million years could she have imagined the magnitude of the secret he'd been holding.

"Is this for the rabids?"

Marcus held on to the answer for a few seconds, as if he was trying to pick the right words. She desperately wanted to urge him on, hurry up the information.

"That wasn't our original intention for it," he finally said. "We were just hoping to find a blood replacement in case…" He paused again, his voice softer. "In case humans became extinct at some point."

The words hit her hard and rocked her to the core. So they were worried about it too. The extinction of the human race. She had been so consumed by the fear of it becoming a reality that she hadn't even thought about the possibility of the vampires worrying about it too. If humans disappeared, vampires were doomed. It was such a simple, basic truth and yet it hadn't even crossed her mind all this time.

It was more than just the realization of what he was saying. It was the sudden understanding that they had a common goal: keep humanity alive and thriving. Maybe the reasons for it were vastly different, but this secret, this lab, could somehow hold the key to the future of humanity.

When she finally spoke, her voice came out shaky. "So this would make us... unnecessary?"

"No," he said before she'd finished speaking. "Even if we figure out how to make this artificial blood work, it's not meant to completely replace humans."

"Why not?"

"Because it will only provide us with nourishment," he said, his voice soft. "Drinking from humans brings other pleasures."

A buzz resonated in her ears before shooting down to her chest and grabbing a hold of her stomach. *Pleasure.* Her mind flashed back to Marcus moaning while rocking inside her, his teeth grabbing a hold of her neck or her inner thigh. The look of ecstasy in his eyes had been as much about her body as about her blood.

She blushed and turned her gaze towards the lab. The puzzled look in the vampire's face was very telling. For whatever reason, she was different. Not only couldn't she be charmed, but all of a sudden she had been given entry to the forbidden kingdom. A kingdom so ancient she could barely manage to grasp bits and pieces of it.

"What about the rabids?"

Marcus and Cyrus exchanged looks, but it was the king who answered. "We don't know yet, but we're hoping the void can be reversed."

The scientist in her took over immediately. "If the void is only caused by a lack of nourishment, rather than by some sort of virus, it should be reversible with enough blood."

Marcus' lips curved up slightly. Almost a smile, but not quite. "And that's why you're here."

CHAPTER 15

He had been waiting to break the news since back in his room. Now that he'd done it, it had just the effect he expected. She froze, her mind clearly going in a million different directions.

"Me?"

He didn't answer right away, partly because he wanted to give her some time to figure it out. But also because Cyrus seemed more than intrigued with Belle and Marcus wanted to make sure limits were set right there, right then. His eyes flashed into darkness for a second, and Cyrus immediately stepped back. It was just a small step, maybe a fraction of an inch—but enough to let him know the lines had been drawn in the sand.

When Marcus turned towards Belle, his eyes were back to a soft silver.

"I was hoping you'd be interested in joining the scientists here at the lab."

A cloak of silence extended over the room. He knew all vampires in the lab had been hanging on to every word of the conversation. Since they could hear him from the other side of the room without any effort, they had all pretended to be focusing on the task in front of them, although he knew for sure the king walking into the room with a human was eventful enough to surpass anything else. Now that he'd stated the actual reason for bringing Belle down there, he could feel the mix of surprise and concern breathing over the space.

"What?" Her voice came out small.

'We need somebody who has a better grasp of human physiology than we do," he said.

Understanding washed over her face. *Beautiful and smart*, he thought. Then he pushed the thought away. *Also fragile as any other human.*

She shook her head and wavered slightly. He immediately extended a hand and grabbed her arm, offering a steady anchor. A soft electric charge passed between them where their skin touched. The effect she had on him still surprised him. He had expected to enjoy her, to feed on her once or twice, and then get bored. But the more time he spent around her, the stronger the connection seemed to become. And that electricity, that whirl of energy that connected them every time they touched… It was just getting stronger by the minute.

It was a sobering realization.

Not only the fact that he was enthralled by a woman this much, but also the fact that the enthrallment was growing, feeding on the energy between them. He suddenly felt very tempted to pull her away from the lab and the hungry eyes around them. An almost uncontrollable need to stake a claim over her, take her back to his room and keep her all to himself.

He ran his hand through his hair and took a deep breath. *Focus.*

Belle's fingers slid over his arm as if they belonged there. It felt like an incredibly intimate gesture, the move of a lover who wasn't afraid of letting others know she belonged to somebody. Or maybe it was just his mind playing tricks on him—in which case he had to believe the warmth exuding from her was also a lie.

"I think... I think I can help," she finally said, and he believed her.

He turned his face towards Cyrus and saw the look of fascination in his eyes. If there was ever any doubt she was Marcus', the last few seconds had to have been confirmation enough. Most of the vampires there had never seen him with a pet, because the few he'd had never been more than that, pets. He was beginning to realize Belle was a lot more. And while her blood was intoxicating—even now, he could smell the excitement running through her veins, making him ache for a taste—it was everything else she was that it was the most intriguing. Not being able to charm her was frustrating, but it also made her superior to others. In a way, it made her closer to him. Impenetrable and unique, that was what Belle was. And the challenge of figuring it all out was proving far more exquisite than he could've dreamt of.

"She'll be safe down here, My Lord," the vampire said and Marcus was glad he didn't have to explain anything else.

He turned to Belle, who was glowing with excitement. This was her turf, what she knew, and probably what she missed.

"Why don't you let Cyrus show you around for a while? They'll escort you up in a couple of hours. See what you can do, if anything, to help." Then he paused for a second and his eyes scouted hers. "Are you sure you want to do this?"

She nodded with resolution. "Oh, yes. There's nowhere else I'd rather be."

He doubted she had meant for the words to hurt him, but they stung anyway. He had a moment of second-guessing himself, where he wondered if giving her space and time away from him was a good idea. The idea bothered him and when he grabbed her arm to let her know the rules, his fingers closed on her skin a little too tight. Sharing her with others wasn't something he wasn't looking forward to, as irrational and insane as that was. But he was also afraid that without a solution, without a touch of magic from somewhere unexpected, the world was running out of options.

It took him a second to realize he was clenching his teeth. He wanted to tell her that she was only allowed down here because he was being generous. Let her know that he had the power to take it all away if he felt her slipping away from his grasp.

Instead, he let go of her arm and took a step back. "Upstairs in three hours," he ordered before disappearing into the darkness of the tunnels.

~*~

Marcus had turned around and stomped out of the lab before she had time to realize what had just happened. Somewhere in the tangle of thoughts rushing through her mind, she had missed something.

"Isabelle," Cyrus interrupted her thoughts. "Let me show you what we have."

She turned around to face the vampire and nodded. She was already in the belly of the beast. *Might as well play along*, she told herself.

"Have you tested the blood?"

Cyrus nodded. "As much as we can in machines." He paused for a second, unsure of what to say next. Or maybe measuring his words as to not say too much. "We've also... tasted it."

The words had no impact on her. Funny that less than a week ago, they would have sent chills down her spine. Now it was just data, numbers and words she was being fed for processing.

"And?"

The vampire looked at her with hesitation. "There's something missing."

She pointed towards the microscope, as if asking for permission. Cyrus nodded and she got closer to take a look through the eyepiece. The cells looked normal—exactly as you would expect from real human blood.

"They look fine to me," she said.

"They do, but they for some reason they don't provide satiation," he said, and then scrambled to find additional words. "We're still hungry after drinking it."

She remembered Marcus words. *Human blood brings other pleasures.* "Could the lack of satisfaction be psychological?"

"No," he said with a light frown. "We thought the same thing at first, but it's more than that. Think of it as being extremely thirsty and drinking water, only to find out it does nothing to quench the thirst."

She looked through the microscope again, searching for any small variation that would indicated a mistake, a failure in the composition. There was none. "Have you played around with the red and white cell blood content?"

"Some. We're trying to stay as close as possible to the original."

She shook her head slightly. "That might be a mistake. Fresh blood is alive, in a way. It contains a certain amount of hemoglobin because we're breathing and that keeps the oxygen flowing at a constant pace. A true substitute, a replacement, might need to account for the difference, especially if you're storing it."

Cyrus' eyes flickered. Then he pointed towards the large refrigerators and storing tubes in the back of the room. "Lead the way," he said.

"This might not work at all, you know," she said.

The vampire shrugged. "We have nothing to lose."

"Fair enough, let's give it a try," she said.

And for the first time in a very long time, it felt like maybe—just maybe—the world had a chance at survival.

CHAPTER 16

That had been a first. Of all the firsts he'd been feeling around Belle, the wave of possessiveness that had hit him down in the lab had been especially powerful. That had been almost two hours ago, and he could still feel the pangs of jealousy surging through his veins. It didn't make any sense, but the truth was that he didn't want to share Belle with anybody. Especially since he didn't truly know if he had enemies inside the compound, vampires plotting his demise behind his back. The kind of enemies who would be happy to hurt Belle just to get to him.

When she came back into his room, he tried to push down the storm raging inside him.

"How did it go in the lab?"

Her eyes had a spark he hadn't seen before. "I think I might actually be able to help," she said. "It looks like—"

He shot to her side before she had time to react, the blur of movements cutting through the room. The truth was that he didn't want to talk right now. He just wanted to take her. Hard, rough, forceful. Right at that moment.

His right hand slid to her neck, fingers encircling her throat gently. Belle gasped but didn't resist him, her heartbeat speeding up to a delirious run. He pushed her against the wall without letting go of her throat. He didn't want to hurt her, but he wanted to make sure she understood who was in charge. His eyes locked on hers, waiting to see if she'd surrender. When she didn't respond, his fingers tightened just a bit and she moaned.

As soon as the sound escaped her throat, his predatory instinct took over, blinding everything else. His body pressed into hers, crushing her tiny figure against the wall behind her. Any hope of softness and control was now gone. He was just an animal trying to mark his prey. He mouth took hers with urgency, his fangs out and trailing her lower lip before his tongue darted into her mouth.

Belle moaned and melted against him, inflaming his need to an almost unbearable point.

His free hand moved behind her, sliding across her ass to cup a cheek. Then he pressed her lower body against his so she could feel his length. The other hand remained where it was around her neck, holding her captive. He wasn't in the mood for foreplay tonight. No gentleness or softness or moving slowly. He wanted—needed—to stake a claim.

His right hand slid from her ass towards the front of her pants, unbuttoning them and sliding them down in a quick movement. And then his pants were down too and he was back pushing against her sex, soft and wet and ready.

Belle looked enthralled, her features heavy with desire. She was panting hard and fast and a cry of almost painful pleasure escaped her throat when he pushed against her.

"You're mine, Belle," he growled, and the words came out deep and weighty.

He could feel his own eyes burning a trail down her throat and then back to her face. There was no fear in Belle's eyes and that only served to drive him even more insane with desire.

He lowered his head down so his lips were almost touching hers. "Tell me you're mine, Belle."

And almost as if he was trying to elicit a response out of her, he adjusted his body so his cock was now at the entrance of her sex. It took every single ounce of willpower he had left not to ram into her right then and there. Instead, he savored the deep moan that escaped her throat. "Tell me," he ordered.

Belle closed her eyes, her body trembling against his. "Yes, yes, I'm yours."

He moved his mouth away from hers and towards his own wrists. When his fangs pierced his skin and the blood started to flow out, Belle's eyes widened. His heart was pounding in his ears and he was mad with need.

He moved his bleeding wrist moved closer to her mouth and Belle's body tensed up in response.

"Marcus, no, what are you doing?" She put her hands up against his chest and tried to push him away but it was too late now, and there was no turning back. He wouldn't allow it.

"Drink," he said, and the words were a mix of order and desire-laden plea.

"No!" He could hear the panic in her voice, but when she tried to shake her head, his fingers tightened on her throat.

He moved his wrist away and pushed against her again, crushing her chest. His hips pushed up and he slid inside her just barely. She was slick and welcoming, her body ready for the invasion. Every inch of his body was throbbing and so was hers.

"It's not going to hurt you," he said, his eyes melting into hers. "You have my word."

And that seemed to work, because Belle's body stopped resisting. He pushed into her a little more and his groan matched hers at the slow torture of the movement. Then he moved his wrist up against her lips again.

"Drink," he ordered softly, and she did.

The second her mouth touched the puncture wounds, he gasped. It felt like a million lightning bolts hitting his body all at once. Pain and urgency and unbelievable ecstasy. His whole body exploded into waves of pleasure and he rammed into her with a grunt. Belle let out a moan and the pressure of her lips on his wrist increased. He let go of her throat and slid a hand down, grabbing her up and off the floor, getting her legs wrapped around him.

Every time he rammed into her, Belle drank harder and moaned louder. The pleasure in her face was exquisite. He could see the orgasm building in her features, grabbing her and twisting her as his own body neared the climax.

And then her tongue darted out and licked the wounds while she continued sucking. That undid him. His whole body bucked, release tearing through him in an almost agonizing wave. Pain and bliss all rolled into one. The most basic, most organic of emotions taking away the last bit of coherence from his mind.

He rammed into her one more time and Belle's body exploded into orgasm. She let go of his wrist, her body arching against his. He held her tight as she rode her own climax, breathless and vibrating in his arms. As she slowly came back to reality, her ragged, harsh breath matched his.

Even if Belle didn't know it yet, they had both just crossed the point of no return.

~*~

Fire. Surging through her veins as if trying to devour her from the inside. Beautiful cold fire lapping through her chest in a hypnotic dance. Even though her body felt spent, she could feel the heat burning its way down her body and into her cells. Vampire blood. It felt wrong and oh-so-right at the same time.

It was the ultimate betrayal, wasn't it? Drinking the blood of the monsters. But the second she had tasted it, something in her had snapped. Nothing she had ever experienced had felt like his blood did. It tasted like honeyed liquor going down her throat and it had ignited a flame inside her, a pang of pleasure that made her want more. Combined with the feeling of him inside her, it became beckoning, like the call of a wild beast.

She adjusted her body against his, trying to find the perfect spot to fall asleep in his arms.

"What's on your mind, Belle?"

You are, she wanted to say. *Always, all the time. You.*

"The blood," she said instead, which was also true. "It felt… empowering."

"What did you expect it to be like?"

"I never asked myself that. I never thought I would…" She took a deep breath. "I guess I imagined it would be… poisonous."

Marcus' face was unreadable.

"No, it has healing properties. And as you saw, sharing it is also highly sexual, which is why we don't usually do it."

The fire moved up towards her face, burning and pulsing in her ears. "Then why…"

"Because it felt right," he interrupted her, grabbing her chin so he could tilt her head slightly back and look into her eyes. "Didn't it?"

Yes, it had. More right than anything she had ever experienced in her life. It had felt like a mix of surrendering and claiming at the same time. As if drinking his blood was making him a part of her, something that could never be erased.

She wanted to deny it, wanted to tell him it had meant nothing. But she didn't have the strength to pretend. Not when his eyes sparkled like silver and the fire of his skin was still against hers.

"Yes," she whispered.

He kissed her, a hint of a wicked smile on his lips. "Of course it did."

Arrogant.

She could feel sleep washing over her, slowly inching its way through her body. It was the kind of soothing sleep she hadn't had for years. The sleep of the satisfied—of the ones who felt safe and content and fulfilled.

And then, halfway between sleep and wakefulness, his body moved against hers. Her skin fluttered and came alive, and she opened her eyes just a bit, hoping to catch sight of him without giving herself away.

The glitter of the moon was dancing on his face, twisting and turning into beautiful shadows over his skin. There was a royal dignity to his presence, a quiet touch of distinction that seemed to ooze out of him even now, as he remained still on the bed next to her. She could deny it all she wanted, but everything he'd done since meeting her had been honorable. All her effort in trying to find the monster hiding in the shadows had been in vain and she was suddenly exhausted from searching for the dark side of him—a side that now she believed maybe didn't exist.

A wave of understanding hit her and hit her hard. And before she could stop it, a thought formed in her mind. *I can't kill him.*

Even if she could find a way to do it, she didn't want to.

Her thoughts flew to the lab and the many surgical tools there. At some point during the night, she'd thought about taking a scalpel back to the room and hiding it in one of her drawers. Then she could have jumped out of the bed and sliced his throat open. She wasn't sure it would kill him and that was a clear sign that her plan had been faulty from the beginning. But none of that mattered because the second she thought about hurting him, a wave of nausea hit her with the intensity of an earthquake. Her breath got caught in her throat and she had to remind herself to try and breathe over the panic that overtook her.

Not only was she sure that she could never hurt him, but she was also suddenly convinced that she would fight anybody who tried. *Tell me you're mine.* Marcus' words echoed in her chest with a thundering boom. Because at that very moment, as his body intertwined with hers on the softness of the blankets, she knew it.

For better or worse, she was his.

CHAPTER 17

She spent most of the following week in the lab. When she wasn't working alongside the scientists, she was spending time in Marcus' bed. Something between them had changed after she'd tasted his blood. There was a deeper connection between them now, a sort of belonging she couldn't ignore anymore—nor did she want to. Over the past few days, she had stopped trying to figure out if feeling this way about the king was a good thing or not.

It was there—a powerful, all-commanding thudding inside her—and she wanted to enjoy it while it lasted. For once, she didn't even care if that made her a traitor.

Besides, her mind was too consumed with everything going on in the lab to worry about anything else when he wasn't around. The scientists were working non-stop to put her ideas into practice. Because they didn't get tired and they could skip sleep if they wanted to, they were always at work. She couldn't keep up with them most of the time and part of her was frustrated that she had to sleep while the lab kept going and the tests continued. She'd even seen Cyrus trying to contain a smile at her annoyance.

Strange how everything could change in a matter of days. From assassin to lover in an instant. And from trying to kill and destroy the vampires to now working to save them.

She didn't want to think about what Shawn would say. He'd been in her mind constantly for the past few days— perhaps because the blood exchange between her and Marcus would horrify her brother. There had been no more rabid attacks on the compound, but the patrols Marcus sent out regularly kept finding them out there. The threat was more alive and closer than ever. And that meant the farm was also in danger. The only family she had left.

While they were making progress in the lab, they still had no answer. So when she came out with the idea of trying out the latest blood sample in a different way, Cyrus was impressed.

Marcus liked the idea a lot less.

"Seems like a very risky move," the king said when he heard her request.

Cyrus seemed ready to back her up, because he intervened before she had a chance to say another word. "It's risky, My Lord, but it could work."

She nodded in agreement. "I know it seems crazy, but I think we've been looking at this the wrong way. Sure, the ultimate goal might be to create something that works for everybody, but it might be wise to start with the rabids." She paused and gave him time to process the concept. "If this works, if the blood substitute cures the rabids, then we know we're on to something. We can work out the kinks out of the formula after that."

Marcus frowned. He obviously wasn't happy with the idea of bringing a rabid into the compound. But it made sense and he had to know that. Bring the beast inside so they could figure out how to cure it—or how to beat it, whatever came first.

"We only need to find a place to keep him so everybody is safe," she added.

Marcus' eyes darkened. "We have cells down here. They'll work."

A shiver ran over her skin. "Cells?"

"I have enemies."

Belle desperately wanted to ask whether the cells were meant for humans or vampires. Deep down, though, she suspected it was for both.

"Are they strong enough to hold a rabid?" she asked.

"They're strong enough to hold ten of them," he answered. Then his expression softened when he looked at her. "Are you sure? This is not going to be comfortable."

She nodded. "I'm sure."

His eyes searched for Cyrus', a question flickering in them.

Cyrus nodded too. "I think she's right, My Lord. This could be the break we've been looking for."

Marcus looked up, almost as if he could see through the ceiling and into the rooms above. "Miles is going to love this."

~*~

It was clear there was nothing Miles loved about the idea, but he knew how to follow orders. All he did was frown slightly and then nod, which was exactly what Marcus had expected him to do.

"How long do you think it will take you to find one?" Marcus asked.

"Finding them is the easy part," Miles said. "It's capturing one alive that might be tricky."

"But possible?"

"Yes, I think so," Miles answered. "Not in Franklin, though. There are too many of them there and we don't want to accidentally start a war."

Marcus leaned against the wall, his whole body tight. Maybe stepping away from the hunt had been a bad idea. He hadn't been outside the compound in a while, so now it was up to his guards to figure out the best route.

"There's an old gas station on the way to Franklin," Miles added. "We found a couple of rabids there last time."

Marcus nodded. "You go and take as many guards as you need. I'll post some guards at the entrance of the tunnels so they can let you in as soon as you get back. Oh, and Miles…"

"Yes?"

"Try to keep the screams under control."

Miles frowned. "I'll try my best."

Marcus watched Miles close the door before he turned around and walked towards the window. He knew there was at least a chance the night was going to get very wild and very loud.

Last time the groups had gone out to search for rabids, they had made sure not to get too close to Franklin. That was because, much to everybody's alarm, Franklin was overrun by rabids. The patrols had found them everywhere—hiding in corners, crouched in the darkness, prying from under staircases and through broken windows. None had come out to attack, probably because there was no human scent around, nothing to get their claws out and fight for. But Jaco had been very clear about what they'd seen: the void was a ticking time bomb just waiting for a spark to explode into flames. The look of madness was spreading and fast. So far, the rabids reaching the compound had probably been flukes, lost ones who had stumbled upon the place. But if the void kept spreading, the smells and lights of the compound would soon become a beacon, attracting every rabid from miles around.

And now they were willingly bringing one of them inside.

Open the door to the devil, his mind chanted.

Might as well start right now.

~*~

She was in the lab when Miles returned with a rabid. She didn't even have to be told what was happening, because she could hear the howling rolling through the tunnels as soon as they got in.

Her breath caught in her throat and she froze. Terrible sounds of agony, of beast-against-beast washed over her. Her heart took off on a race, fueled by a mix of anticipation and paralyzing fear.

The real monsters are out there. Thanks to her, they were now inside as well.

She turned around to look at Cyrus.

He seemed to gather his thoughts before he got up from his work station and made his way towards her. "Let's just wait," he said. And she knew he meant, *Let's just wait for the king.*

They didn't have to wait long, because Marcus was down in the lab in what seemed like seconds. The instant the door opened, his eyes searched for her. Once he locked on her, his whole body seemed to settle. She moved closer, the screams still resonating down the hallways and reverberating in her ears. Her mind kept playing images of the rabid escaping and finding his way to the lab, to the only human down in the bowels of the beast. She tried to push the picture away, but the sounds of agony cutting through the silence of the tunnels were too terrifying to ignore.

He's coming for you, her mind taunted her. She closed her eyes and took a deep breath.

"We'll wait until it's secure in the cell before going over," he told her, and she could hear the hesitation in his voice.

"I'm fine," she said.

"Like hell you are," he whispered.

She looked up and into his eyes. There was genuine concern there and it tugged at her. "I'll be fine," she corrected, and then she added, "Just stay close."

He extended a hand and grabbed hers just as she heard a clank in the distance. Metal doors banging shut. "I'm not going anywhere," he said and then started walking towards the door, tugging her along.

After being inside the lab and surrounded by bright lights for a couple of hours, the darkness of the tunnels seemed even more gripping than usual. She'd started to get used to trampling through the tunnels without lights, but only because the last few days she'd been going in and out of the lab constantly. She always had a guard with her, mainly because the tunnels were a labyrinth of fake walls and unexpected turns she couldn't decipher on her own. At one point she'd asked about a flashlight but had been told it was best to keep the tunnels in the dark. Whether it was to avoid being seen by potential enemies or to keep her from seeing what lurked in the darkness, she didn't know. She suspected it was probably a bit of both.

But tonight, the tunnels were just as terrifying as the first time she had stepped into them. This time, it was because she knew what was waiting for them at the other end of the walk. Marcus' fingers were tight on hers and she was glad for the touch, the warmth spreading up through her arm with a soft electrical buzz.

As they got closer to the rabid, the howls got louder and louder. It was a deep haunting sound that she could only describe as the sound of desperation. The thuds of a frantic beast that found itself caged. The sound of sickness. It could have been sad if it wasn't terrifying. Her whole body screamed for her to run the other way. Marcus must have sensed her fear, because he tightened his grip on her hand.

"Stay away from the cage, Belle," he said as they reached their destination. "He's going to go crazy when he sees you."

She swallowed hard, reality sinking like a stone in her already queasy stomach.

"Right," she said, only because she was having a hard time coming up with words.

And then he pushed the door open. It took less than a second for the rabid to realize there was a human in the room, and then all hell broke loose. The rabid threw its body against the door, banging with such force it seemed like the whole room shook in response. She jumped backwards, part of her fearing the door would give. But it didn't, so the rabid pounced on it again and again and again, oblivious to anything but the human scent attacking its senses. It picked up speed in between bangs, until everything became a blur of momentum and sound lurching around the cell.

It reminded her of a caged animal. There was truly no other way of describing it. She could barely see its features because of the speed of the movements, but there were flashes of skin and blood and agony blazing in front of her eyes.

She couldn't imagine what it was like, suffering from hunger so frantic that it consumed you. Through the years, she'd seen what hunger could do to humans, but she'd never experienced it to an extreme. To the point where madness was the only possible outcome.

"Belle?" Marcus' fingers moved over hers.

The voice brought her back to reality. "Can we sedate it?"

The rabid started howling again, a mix of pain and despair that sent a shiver down to her bones. Bang against the metal door. Howl. Bang again. The more time she spent there, the louder the room became.

"Miles, get Cyrus here," Marcus said, and only then she realized there were other vampires in the room.

Miles' clothes were covered in blood, part of his shirt torn to reveal cuts and scrapes on the skin underneath. Her whole body inched forward, the doctor in her ready to help. But Miles raised a hand to wave her off, guessing her intentions. "I'm fine," he said. "The wounds will heal on their own in a matter of hours."

Her eyebrows went up, curiosity pricked. "That easily?"

Marcus let go of her hand and moved towards the cell. Next to the rabid, he oozed serenity. It was a startling disparity seeing the two vampires face to face: the quiet dignity of the king and the madness of the beast in front of him. Just how easily one could morph into the other? "You'll get a chance to figure out how resilient we are," Marcus said, his eyes locked on the rabid.

The beast stopped its maddening spell for a few seconds, just long enough for Belle to see the blood dripping, its injuries bright red against its blackened sick skin.

By the time Miles returned with Cyrus, the howling madness had become almost unbearable. Her whole body was now pulsating along with the sounds, the screams grinding down into her bones until it hurt.

Still, when Miles and Marcus reached into the cage to hold the rabid down so Cyrus could inject it, her heart hammered in terror. She waited for a few seconds for the tranquilizer to take effect and when it didn't, Cyrus injected the rabid again.

"How much?" she asked.

"Enough to knock down an elephant or two," Cyrus responded.

When she tried to step towards the cage, Marcus put his hand up to stop her. "Let's tread carefully here, Belle. We don't know much about their bodies and how they work. I don't want it to wake up and find you just inches away from the door."

A shiver shot through her. No, she certainly didn't want that either. So she waited for a couple of minutes, her breath frozen while observing the creature spread on the ground inside the cell. It was a sobering sight and hard to believe the beast had once been as magnificent as the other vampires in the room. Now, it looked like a completely different species. The skin was darkened. Burned, maybe? It was possible, she guessed, that it had spent time in the sun and ended up with charred skin as a result.

But it was more than that. The ashy coloring of the skin seemed the color of sickness, as if the blood running under the surface had blackened and scorched the skin along with it.

Even though its eyes were closed at the moment, they still appeared sunken, as if they were slowly being absorbed back into the skull. And its face seemed hollow as well, the skin tight and dry against the bone.

In its quiet drugged sleep, the rabid didn't look as a fearless beast; instead, it just looked sick.

"Cyrus," she said. "Can we get some blood from him? A few vials. Maybe some skin samples?"

Cyrus moved quickly, getting what she needed. When the rabid twitched in its drugged stupor, the scientist jerked his hands away and waited for stillness before he resumed searching for a vein. "I think we might want to keep him sedated at all times," he said. "Otherwise, he's going to be screaming nonstop, day and night."

Miles looked at the rabid and then Marcus. "We could bring the UV lamps here."

She looked at both of them with hesitation. "UV lamps?"

Marcus frowned slightly. "If we turn them on the rabid, the light will weaken it. Make it less feral."

She winced. "Won't that burn? Hurt?"

There was a hint of wonder in the king's eyes. "It will hurt. A lot. But it won't kill it as long as we keep the voltage low."

Belle shook her head. There was something intrinsically wrong with the idea. Sure, the thing inside the cell was a monster. But it was a monster because it was sick. Without the pestilence running through its veins, it might have been as magnificent as the vampires around her.

She didn't even want to dwell on those thoughts. A month ago, all vampires had been monsters in her mind. But right now, the pieces on the chessboard had moved. Suddenly, they each had their own strategic place: the king, the knights, the pawns. And the rabids had become the opponent on the other side of the board. One false move and it was checkmate.

For all of them.

The thing was, she would much rather fix the sick than exterminate them. It wasn't just a question of being noble—it was also about practicality. Because killing or torturing a rabid here and there would make no difference: the void would keep spreading and putting the few remaining humans in danger. But if they could figure out a cure and in the process also find a way to feed the vampires, maybe they all had a fighting chance.

She would sooner do all of that without any pain in the process. There had been enough pain already.

"I'd rather not do that," she finally said.

There was something unsettling about the intensity in Marcus' eyes gliding over her. She expected words to come out of his mouth, but he just stood there for what seemed like hours, a stilled expression on his face. Then he turned around to look at Cyrus. "Do we have enough tranquilizers to keep him like this for a while?"

"It depends on how fast he wakes up," Cyrus said. "Maybe a few days, maybe a week."

And then what? She shuddered at the idea. "Let's move fast, then."

The look on Cyrus' face confirmed it. Wasting time was not an option.

CHAPTER 18

Every time he saw Belle at work, in her element, something inside him stirred. It momentarily erased her humanity and made her stronger, larger, more of an equal. And that was when his mind started to run with the idea of making her a partner. *Keep her.* He had no idea how. Make her a vampire? There hadn't been a female vampire in centuries and even if he took the risk of turning her into one, he wasn't sure she would go along with the idea.

He wasn't even sure how she felt about him.

The only thing he was sure about was that Belle was keeping secrets. He could see it in her eyes now and then. When desire took over, when she truly surrendered to the connection between them, the real Belle was raw and passionate and a force impossible to ignore. But at other times, when they were surrounded by his kind or out "into the world," she was guarded. She looked like she was processing information, safeguarding it for later on.

Jaco and Grayson had been keeping tabs on her during the day, following her every move. Part of Marcus hated spying on her, but part of him couldn't resist the idea of knowing what drove her. She didn't seem to have any friends at the compound. In fact, after a few days of consorting with one other female, she had seemed to lose interest and now spent most of her time either walking around the compound or surrounded by other vampires.

In a way, she seemed to be more at ease around his kind than she was around humans. Even if she wasn't aware of it, she fit in well. Minutes ago, when she had refused to harm the rabid using a UV lamp, he could feel the wave of compassion extending through the room. He had been ready to hurt the rabid, and she—a human who had every right to want to kill the beast—had spoken in its favor. The whole world was turning a corner right in front of his eyes.

But that didn't answer the questions he had, like where she had come from and what she had left behind. It wasn't something she wanted to talk about, which probably meant she had much to say—but was choosing not to.

Whatever connection there was between them, it wasn't strong enough for her to betray her secrets—so he had let it go, despite his curiosity.

Right now, as she was scrambling around the lab, the questions were back in his mind. *Who are you, Belle?*

She looked through the eyepiece on the microscope, then retreated back for a couple of seconds before moving forward to look again.

"What is it?" he asked her.

"I don't know. I've never seen blood like this before. It seems… slow."

"What does that mean, slow?"

Cyrus seemed to understand exactly what she was saying. "The cells, they don't behave like normal cells. They respond slowly, as if they're dying." He paused for a second. "Which they are, I guess."

She nodded. "I need healthy blood to compare it to this. Healthy vampire blood, I mean. I know what mine looks like."

A blanket of silence fell over the lab and he knew why. Sharing vampire blood was not something they took lightly. Especially when a human was involved. There had been a lot of blood shed at the hand of human hunters, and over the centuries, vampire blood had become almost sacred. *Never give it willingly. Fight to the death to protect it.* Even though the circumstances were different, he could understand the hesitation.

He stepped forward, rolling up the sleeves of his shirt. "Take it."

Alarms went off in every single vampire in the room. He could hear their hearts pounding in response, the halted breath in a few of them.

"My Lord, it's not necessary..." Cyrus said, and his voice sounded tight.

He raised a hand to stop him. "It's fine." And then his eyes moved towards the only human in the room. "Isn't it, Belle?"

She nodded, her heart pounding deliciously against her ribs. The sound was almost musical to his ears. Enticing and warm.

The dead silence in the room got even deeper when she pressed the needle against his skin. As the blood started to flow into the syringe, Belle's heart sped up, her breath slightly faster and more ragged. He blinked, trying to control the surge of heat flowing through his body, but the images of her sucking on his wrist were too powerful to ignore. His whole body woke up and Belle must have felt it, because her breath quickened to match the mood.

She looked up and glanced at him, their eyes meeting in an exchange of understanding. "That's… enough…" she managed to whisper and there was a throbbing cadence to her voice.

When he moved his eyes away, it was obvious that every vampire in the room had caught the exchange. The sharp look in Miles' eyes was clear enough, but the other vampires also seemed awestruck with the understanding of what had just transpired in the room. Belle's heart was still pounding, and the sound alone was luscious enough to tell the whole story. The secret was out.

Her eyes were back on the eyepiece, but her hands were trembling slightly.

"Oh," she said then, and the simple word echoed through the room like a hurricane.

"What is it?" Marcus asked.

"The blood; it's just the opposite of the rabids'. Incredibly fast-moving, as if the cells keep…" And then her whole face lit up. "Reproducing. That's what it is, isn't it?" She looked up to him. "You said vampire blood had healing properties. It's because the cells reproduce so fast, that they take over and heal whatever else it's in there. That's why…"

Her words stopped, but he knew what she wanted to say: that was why she had felt so energized after drinking his. And suddenly he knew what she was going to say next. Because it made sense. And because she had no idea what she was asking, so she wasn't afraid to put the words out there.

"Maybe we need to add some vampire blood to the mix. Maybe that's what the fake blood is missing," she said.

That was exactly what he thought she was going to say. And the look of horror on every vampire in the room was just as profound as he'd expected it to be too.

_*_

The second she'd let the words out, the air in the room thickened. She was sure the vampires had caught at least part of the implicit exchange between her and the king when she took his blood. But now that she'd said the words out loud, it felt like a shroud of death had fallen over everything and everybody.

All she knew was that it made sense. If vampire blood could heal, maybe it could mend the sick cells rushing through the rabids' bodies. Cyrus would understand this much better than her, but in theory, all it would take was a few drops of vampire blood to maybe make a difference. Except that the doom in the air around her made it seem like she was asking them to kill or torture somebody.

"What is it?" she finally asked.

"Vampire blood is poisonous to other vampires," Marcus explained.

She shook her head, looking around the room to find some support. "What about to rabids? Has anybody tried it?"

"We don't share our blood," Cyrus said.

Her eyes flew to Marcus, whose arms were crossed over his chest. He looked magnificent with his sleeves rolled up, the muscles in his arms flexed and cut to perfection. There was a spark of mischief in his eyes, almost as if he was daring her to get out of the situation on her own.

"Not even for somebody of your same species?" she asked, and while it was a question meant for everybody, her eyes stayed frozen on the king.

"There's been a lot of blood lost through our history," he finally said. "Mostly at the hands of humans, but also from vampire traitors."

A huge knot settled in her stomach. "I… didn't know…"

"Sharing blood has become off limits," Miles added from the back of the room. "A ritual reserved for few and with great meaning."

She wavered, swallowing hard. Marcus' eyes were sparkling with a force that was nearly audible. What he had shared with her, what had happened in his bedroom that night, it had been more than just pleasure and passion for him. He had opened up to her, given her a glimpse into the immortal world.

He shed blood for me.

The tightness in her stomach extended upwards, squeezing her chest with the intensity of an iron fist.

"We need to try," she whispered. "We already have a rabid here so there's nothing to lose."

Marcus stood quiet for a second, glaring at her. Then he turned around slowly, as if he was trying to make an impression. When his eyes reached Cyrus, the scientist winced slightly. They were all afraid of him, she realized. Or wary, at least, careful not to move or say the wrong thing. "Can you make this work?" Marcus asked him.

Cyrus' face twisted with a mix of disgust and understanding. "What she's saying makes sense, sir. The void might cause the cells to become sick, so they can no longer heal themselves. That would explain the mental deterioration as well."

"It's like dementia," she added. "Neurons slowly lose their capacity to function. They deteriorate, causing multiple system atrophy…" She stopped and took a deep breath, trying to find simpler words. "Your brain degrades until it stops working rationally."

Marcus' eyes returned to her. "How much of our blood?"

"I don't know," she said, eyeing the tiny drops on the stage of the microscope. "Maybe just a few drops, maybe more. We can start with the smallest amount possible and go up from there."

She knew she was asking a lot, but at this point, the experiment was as much for the benefit of the vampires as it was for the human race. If they didn't find a cure—and soon—the void would keep expanding, taking over daylight until there was no safe time and place for any of them.

Marcus nodded, a determination in the gesture that left no doubt of his decision. "OK, let's give it a try."

And despite the overwhelming feeling of disapproval that rocked the room, nobody said a word. She guessed that contradicting the king wasn't really an option.

She adjusted her weight on the chair, feeling the tension in her back getting deeper. Exhaustion was slipping down into her bones, slowing her body down. It had been a long day, and now that the adrenaline was starting to wear off, her body was begging her to lie down.

"Why don't you take a break, Belle?" Marcus said from behind her. "Cyrus can get this started and you can join him back in the morning."

She shook her head. "No, I want to be here."

Cyrus took a step forward, a hint of a smile forming on his face. "I promise not to do anything groundbreaking without you here. Let us do the background work while you sleep."

She wanted to say no, but her body was fighting her. She had been sleeping less and less lately, trying to keep up with the immortals around her. It was frustrating to have to take breaks while everybody else was still working and feeling as strong and awake as ever.

But right now—and despite how much she wanted to be there—a bed sounded like heaven.

"OK," she conceded.

Cyrus was already back to work before she had time to turn around and leave.

CHAPTER 19

The second she stepped into her bedroom, she realized she'd left her notes behind in the lab. She wanted to take a quick bath before getting into bed, and the only way to do that and not end up in Marcus' arms was to do it in her own bedroom. With him around, the temptation to touch was just too great.

She knew he probably had other things on his mind anyway. The exchange back in the lab had left a lot of questions unanswered, but one thing was clear: she had touched on a taboo subject and she suspected he wanted to discuss it—if not with all vampires, at least with those closer to him.

Not that her mind wasn't a raging chaos too. She desperately wanted to ask him why but all the way back through the tunnels and into her room, she had resisted the urge. Maybe because part of her was afraid of what the answer would be. Right now, the question was back, pulsing in her temples, firing up the blood throbbing in her ears. *Why?* Why share with her something so special? Why break a code he'd been carrying around for centuries?

She had a massive headache and all she wanted was to get into the bathtub with her notes and forget about how Marcus made her feel. As much as possible, anyway, and just for a few hours. Except that she had left the paperwork back at the lab. She sighed and looked towards the door that separated her bedroom from Marcus. Either she had to ask him to guide her through the tunnels and back into the lab, or she could walk outside and try to open the false door they had used the first time they went underground.

She decided she needed the fresh air and solitude anyway, so she stepped outside and into the courtyard.

The night was quiet. Over the past few years, wildlife had grown considerably and the night hunters like coyotes and wolves now roamed the land in numbers greater than ever before. But that night, even they were quiet. A soft breeze carried the promise of rain in it; she took a deep breath, hoping to catch a hint of wetness in the air, before she closed the door behind her.

The second she turned the corner towards the dead-end corridor and the false door, she caught a glimpse out of the corner of her eye. A quick shadow flashing past. Her heart sped up and for a terrifying moment, she thought it might be a rabid. But the rabids were shrill and careless in their movements, too desperate to maintain the grace of old vampires gliding through the air.

You're imagining things, she told herself. But even then, she didn't believe it. She swallowed hard and took another step. And then she heard the soft snapping sound to her right.

She wasn't stubborn or stupid enough to ignore that. It was probably just one of Marcus' guards, keeping tabs on her, but it seemed... wrong somehow. As if the sounds didn't belong there.

She was about to turn around when steps resonated behind her. Steps too light to be human but too obvious for a vampire trying to hide his presence. Steps with a purpose.

"Well, well."

The familiar voice was so unexpected, for a second she thought she had to have imagined it. Then she heard the slightest of steps forward and her whole body froze into place. Cold spikes of fear burrowed into her spine and slid down into her chest, squeezing until she found herself fighting for breath.

"So you made it here after all," he said, and the delight in his voice was palpable.

It took what felt like long minutes for her body to move. The chill traveling down her spine took hold of her legs, freezing her feet to the ground. The air around her suddenly seemed thick with darkness and a humming of danger rippled strongly all the way down to her bones. She took a deep breath before she turned around to find vampire eyes locked on her.

Eyes she knew well from back in the factory.

He was smiling, his face dark among the shadows. Her eyes darted to the sides, looking for a way out, even though it was obvious he was blocking the only entrance to the courtyard. Her door, all the way down the side of the building, seemed miles away.

"Nowhere to go," he taunted her, and the ripple of fear extended deeper.

Her feet slid backwards, even though she knew she was just pushing herself into a corner. He was still, just as he had been back at the factory. She understood then it was all part of the game: stare your prey down until it cowers in fear and you can slay it with a single pounce. It was all part of the fun.

His smile widened, his eyes almost playful as he watched her panic grow larger.

"Want to play before I kill you?" he whispered as he moved forward, and the idea of another vampire touching her made her stomach turn.

Time froze. She felt herself suspended at the edge of the abyss, fear waiting for the perfect moment to push her down. She could scream—but the vampire in front of her would be on her before help could materialize. The rumble of thunder crashed overhead and the breeze picked up and whirled around her. The sounds of a dead night.

A chill spread through her, causing her heart to boom and pound—a noise that no doubt he found enticing.

"I think your king wouldn't be very happy if you did that," she managed to whisper through the knot in her throat.

It was a desperate attempt to keep him engaged and maybe gain some time.

The vampire's laugh resonated in the empty courtyard. "Is that so?"

"Isabelle's right."

Her heart skipped a beat when Marcus's voice came from behind her, relief and warmth surging through her. How had he gotten there? Another secret door?

Marcus stepped into the light, his massive form shrinking the darkness around her. She listened to her own heart change beats as he leaned forward and locked his eyes on hers. His eyes were the color of charcoal, deep and dark and dangerous.

"Are you OK?"

The unexpected softness in his voice was racking. She nodded before turning her head back towards the intruder.

The intruder stepped forward. His smile was gone and he was obviously unhappy, either to find the king there or because he'd lost the chance to get his hands on her.

"What's this? Is your majesty taken by a human?" The mix of surprise and irritation at losing his prey was buzzing in the air.

"Why are you here, Patrick? You were told you weren't welcome."

Marcus's arm extended sideways to grab her and push her behind him, shielding her.

"Is that how you welcome your brother after so long?"

The words hit her hard, making her gasp. Brother? It couldn't be. She searched for a touch of resemblance in their features and couldn't find any. Patrick looked like a predator. No warmth in his face, no hint of passion. Just eyes the color of the night.

The entire courtyard was alive with the energy hissing between the two vampires. So intense it was just about visible. She could feel the fight about to break and her whole body stiffened in anticipation.

"How about sharing?" the intruder whispered, and Marcus's body tensed, his back turning into stone.

"No. And I want you out."

The vampire took a step backwards casually, without losing his smile.

"Just passing by. But not for the last time." His eyes moved towards her and she caught a glimpse of his fangs, fully extended. "See you soon, brother. You too, darling."

Patrick jumped up, almost as if he was about to walk on the wall. He moved too fast for her to realize what was happening. A half second, the blink of an eye, and he was gone over the wall and into the darkness outside the compound.

Marcus' body was still a rock and when her hands grazed his back, his muscles twitched and clenched under her touch. Then he turned around to face her, his fangs still out. He looked ready for war. As soon as he locked his eyes with her, however, his face softened. Only then did she realize her legs were shaking.

"I think I need to sit down."

"Inside," he told her.

He touched the wall behind them and a door opened. Another door that shouldn't be there. He gently pushed her through the short passageway before opening the second door into his bedroom.

She reached the bed just in time before her knees collapsed.

"Is he really your brother?"

Marcus frowned. "He's more than that. He's been wanting the throne for centuries. And for the first time, I now have a weak spot he can target."

She could see the tension in his beautiful face. "What's that?"

"You," he said and Isabelle's world turned upside down.

She remained still, silent, waiting for him to correct himself. But he just stood there, his eyes melting back into a silvery grey. "What…?"

"Truth time," he said softly, but it sounded like an order. "You first."

And she decided she wanted to give in. No more lies, no more hiding. There was no point and she was tired. And the prospect of Patrick taking over as the king was more terrifying than anything she could imagine.

"How do you know Patrick?" He nudged her to start talking.

Blood drained away from her face. "On my way here, from… I ran into him. It wasn't pleasant."

He shook his head. "How did you get away?"

"The sun was coming up… Or at least I thought that was the reason at the time…" She hesitated. "I don't think he knows he can't charm me."

"Did he touch you?" he muttered, a hint of suppressed rage in his voice.

"No, he didn't have a chance."

He groaned. "But now he knows I care about you and he'll do whatever he can to use that against me."

The words resonated in her chest. "You care? As in 'don't kill my pet' care?"

He shot her a dry look. "No, Belle." He crouched in front of her and grabbed her hands. "Isn't it obvious I care about you? Seems fitting that after a few hundred years of being alone, I end up falling for a human."

Isabelle's heart contracted, then took off on a mad race. The world turned and twisted around her and inside her. She was sure she was supposed to say something at that moment, but she couldn't come up with any words. The buzzing in her ears intensified. "You... it can't be."

One of his hands moved sideways, grabbing the back of her thigh in a move both comforting and possessive. "Why? Because I'm supposed to be a monster?"

She exhaled, her soul surrendering. It was a lost battle, trying to deny how she felt. It had been a lost battle for a long time—maybe from the time he touched her. She had been denying her feelings because they seemed like a betrayal to the entire human race, but denying them was a betrayal to her own soul.

The night got darker and deeper as the first spatters of rain hit the window.

"Because I'm supposed to hate you," she finally conceded.

He gave her a pointed look, his eyes unreadable in the silence of the room. "And do you?"

The storm outside matched the one raging on inside her. She felt the urge to open a window, let the storm in to embrace them both—but she didn't move.

"I've tried... I... No." She took a deep breath. "Remember a while ago, when I said I was yours?"

The silver in his eyes seemed to sparkle with unread emotions. "Yes," he said.

"I meant it," she finally said and as the words came out, relief washed over her.

Marcus straightened up, his hand reaching for the back of her head. When his lips closed on hers, there was a gentleness there that brought tears to her eyes. The warmth of his touch spread over her and her chest contracted.

"I came here to kill you," she said when he finally broke the kiss.

He inched away and stayed silent, waiting for her words.

"You... humankind is more or less gone. We were hoping to rebuild, survive somehow. We thought maybe if the king was dead, it would help. I don't know."

"And you were the appointed killer?"

"It was my idea."

He got up and turned around, walking a few steps, away from her and towards the window. "What now?"

What now? The question thundered around in her head. She had no answer for that. "I don't know, Marcus. Everybody I love is suffering, hiding, fading away... I don't want them to die."

He turned around to face her. He had never looked more human and more magical than he did at that moment. "Even if you could kill me, that would only open the door for Patrick to take over."

She got up, stumbling slightly. Her legs were slowly returning to normal. "I don't want you to die anymore."

He smiled his half smile. "Well, that's a relief."

She shook her head. "It doesn't make any sense, Marcus. It's not like we can truly be together and pretend we're the same. Or pretend the world isn't dying around us. I don't even know who… what… you really are."

He moved with the speed of lightning, materializing in front of her before she even realized he had moved. "You mean things like this?" He grabbed her chin and pushed her head slightly backwards so he could lock eyes with her. "It's all an illusion, Belle. It doesn't really matter." He noticed her trying to speak and he placed a finger on her lips to prevent it. "But I can answer any questions you have."

Questions. She had a world of them. And now that she had told him the truth about her presence in the compound, she was finally free to ask them. Except that suddenly, she didn't care. She just wanted to stay there, close to him, pretending the world outside didn't exist.

He smiled. "Well?"

His fingers traced her face, as if he was savoring the memory of her skin. It was almost easy to forget he wasn't human in moments like those. Almost. Because deep down, there was a war raging in her soul. There was no way she could keep denying what she felt for him. And yet she also couldn't deny what that meant for everybody else out there, counting on her to do something.

She swallowed hard. "I want to know why me? Where are the female vampires?"

Marcus rubbed his neck. "I don't have a real answer for the first question, Belle. There's something special about you."

"Because you can't charm me?"

"That's only part of it," he said. "I guess you could say I was intrigued from the beginning. And that's not something that happens often."

"What about my other question?"

"There haven't been any female vampires since the sixteenth century," he said. "We had a big outbreak of the void and it affected the females of our species much more rapidly. There haven't been any female vampires since then."

A chill ran through her. "So you've been without a partner all this time?"

His eyes probed into hers. "Until now."

She let the words wash over her. There was a roughness to him that she respected—the kind that came from suffering and surviving. The kind she felt too. So hearing him confess that he also felt something at the other end of the spectrum was a revelation. One that was just as unexpected as it was welcomed.

He lay down on the bed and signaled for her to come along. Before she moved, before she let him touch her, there was one thing she needed to know. Something only he could answer.

"What about the rest of the world?"

He didn't ask the obvious "what about it" follow-up question. He didn't blink or look confused or try to ignore the reality behind her words.

"How much do you know?" he asked instead.

She shook her head, a cold shiver finding her way down her spine and into her chest.

"Not much. Communications were down before we got details of what was happening in other countries."

He studied her face for a moment. "Some countries held on longer than others. We're still fighting small pockets of resistance in Europe. Some. Here and there." He paused, probably waiting for her to absorb the impact of the revelation. "It's over, Belle. Unless there's some secret conspiracy being set up somewhere, we don't expect things to change."

It's over. Humanity, the chance for a return to "normal," a future… Over.

"How many are left?"

She couldn't push herself to use the word "humans."

"I don't know. A few million, spread over the world. It wasn't just the invasion that killed so many humans. Many killed each other after, or died of disease or starvation. I suspect there are many more like you, hiding away and waiting for the right moment to surface."

More like her. Planning something impossible and then failing to even try anyway.

They talked for hours that night. About his past, the history of his kind, and the wars he'd seen and fought. About the dreams he had of a peaceful Earth and how exterminating the human race had never been his intention. He offered no excuses or apologies. Instead, he told her the truth about how he'd planned on becoming the ruling species and somehow finding a way to make it work for humans. She cringed at the words but part of her understood. His species had been around longer than hers. For most of that time, they had lived a life of misery, hiding and surviving as they could, hunted and persecuted. She hated the idea with a passion but in reality, they probably had more of a right to the planet than humans did. It didn't excuse the killing, the hunting and the near extermination of the human race.

It excused nothing.

But she understood all the same because she could hear the honesty in his voice.

He'd lived a long life, and while there was a lot of magnificence to it, there was also a lot of pain. Death had been a constant companion. Because she had never thought of vampires as sentient beings before, she had never realized just how much misery you could truly experience through centuries of living in hiding. Five years of living that way had taken a toll on her and those she loved. What would it be like to live a hundred years that way? Two hundred? Always hiding, always searching for food and hoping you'd find some without being discovered. The idea was too horrible to even consider.

She believed every word he told her. In fact, she felt the pain and fever and world-weariness behind every one of those words.

Sometime during the night, he called Miles in to let him know of the break-in. There was no doubt that whoever was letting the rabids in had also let Patrick slip through. Even Isabelle could see that. And the walls had been conveniently unguarded so the vampire could jump in and out without being discovered.

The two vampires talked for just a few minutes while she lay on Marcus' bed, tangled in the covers. When he came back over to the bed, he traced a finger over her face. "Seems like the rabids are not our only problem anymore."

She frowned. "And seems like there's been a lot of break-ins lately."

He switched positions on the bed, lying on his back and drawing her along with him. "I noticed that too."

Chapter 20

Belle finally fell asleep in his arms sometime before dawn. He stayed with her, mostly because he was afraid to move and wake her up. She looked exhausted and he felt somewhat guilty because he had been keeping her up at night—either by bringing her into his bed or by taking her to the lab. Not that she needed to be dragged either place—she was more than willing to undress and always eager to head to the lab.

He couldn't blame her. Now that he knew why she had made her way into the compound, he could blame her even less.

What the hell was he supposed to do with her confession? He'd always known she was keeping secrets, just not which ones. Now he had to wonder whether there were other humans out there with the same objective: hunt the king down and kill him. The kind of humans he would have to execute with a blow, maybe even in front of her.

He looked down at her face, soft and serene against his chest. She was right about one thing: they were worlds apart. He was ready to fight anything and anybody to protect her, but that didn't change his priorities: save the vampire race. Humans—all except the one in his arms right at that moment—were secondary. He still needed them to stay alive, but maybe even that need would disappear soon enough.

And then what?

Then there was also Patrick and the rabids.

He looked up towards the window. The first hints of daylight were filtering through the drawn curtains. Rain had stopped a few hours ago but he could still smell the dampness in the air.

The night hunters would soon go back into their sleeping hideouts. All of them except the rabids, who would venture into the light, looking to surprise their prey. And while he wasn't planning on stepping under the sunlight, he was planning on staying up and heading towards the lab with Belle as soon as she woke up.

And once that was under control, he was planning on going out, finding Patrick and skinning him alive.

It was time for his brother to die.

~*~

She woke up to feel Marcus' arms tight around her. Images and words from the night before slowly rolled into her mind. She'd crossed a line she couldn't undo—and now that the sun was up, she had no choice but to deal with it.

"How are you feeling?"

Hard to pretend anything with vampire senses around. Marcus could probably sense the slight changes in her breathing or her heartbeat as she woke up. *How am I feeling? I have no idea.* She was glad there were no secrets between them anymore.

"Still shaken, somewhat. The light doesn't bother you?" She pointed towards the sunshine spilling into the room. It touched parts of the floor and the walls and grazed one of the pillars of the bed. It was just a tiny fleck of light and she would have completely ignored it at any other time, but it unnerved her right now. Too close to vampire skin.

"Not really, no," he said. "As long as I don't stretch my hand into it. About last night…"

"What about it?" she said, hoping he wouldn't want to revisit anything of what was said just hours before. For some reason, repeating any of it during daylight seemed a lot harder and a lot less real. She wanted time to digest everything, to figure out where to go from there. What she now was—and wasn't—anymore.

"Why were you outside?"

"What?"

"You were outside, alone, when Patrick found you. Why?"

She didn't like where the conversation was going, but she especially didn't like the undertones in Marcus' voice.

"Trying to find my way back to the lab," she answered. "I left something behind."

"You're not supposed to be out on your own."

She jumped out of the bed. "I'm not *supposed to*? You said I wasn't a prisoner."

"When did I say that?"

She turned around to face him, fire building up inside her. "When I first got here, you said people here were free to come and go."

"People, yes. Not you. Not anymore."

"What does that mean, not me?"

Marcus got up and reached for her, but she jerked her arm away. He anticipated the movement—or he was just fast enough to react to it—and he caught her anyway. Then he let her go a second later, probably because he noticed the fury in her eyes.

"Belle, I can't risk you putting yourself in danger. I get it, you're strong. You survived a night on the roads. But things have changed. Next time Patrick comes face to face with you, he's going to tear you to pieces. Because of who you are, because of me."

A shiver ran over her skin. He was right, of course, but that didn't make his words any easier to swallow. "I didn't know that last night."

"No, but you knew about the rabids breaking into the compound."

"What about everybody else?"

"What about them? My guards are doing their best to keep the compound safe, but the only one I'm truly concerned about is you."

The unspoken words in Marcus' eyes were almost audible. *To hell with everybody else*, he was saying. If it came to it, there was no doubt he would walk away from every human in the compound and let them die.

"So they don't matter, all the people here?" She heard herself saying the words but still felt a pang of sadness as they resonated in the room.

"I'll protect them if I can, but they're not my priority. You are. The vampires in this compound are."

"How generous of you," she scoffed.

And she realized that was the dark side of him she had been waiting to see. His true vampire side. He was still one hundred percent loyal to his species—and the reason it bothered her so much was that she had been slowly turning her back on hers.

The people back at the farm could all be dead for all she knew. And her major worry today had been whether the sun might touch him.

Traitor, her mind singsonged.

"I'm ready to go back to the lab," she said, turning around and walking away from him.

"Belle, let's talk about this."

She didn't want to look at him for fear of breaking down, of the words getting to her. "Let's just go."

And to her surprise, he said nothing else and instead led her directly to the secret door on the opposite side of the room.

She stepped through it and darkness enveloped her. Because she refused to grab his hand, it took longer than usual to reach the lab. It was a childish reaction, refusing his help, but she didn't care. She didn't want to be touched because she wanted to forget—at least for a while—just how good his touch felt. It was hard to be angry with him when he felt so good.

She stumbled for the first few feet through the tunnel, but after a while, the screams of the rabid became clear. They sounded muffled, drugged out into the distance, but they were loud enough to serve as a beacon. The bellowing traveling down the corridors wasn't as loud as the night before, so the rabid was either still half-dazed from the night before or Cyrus had had to give him another round of tranquilizers. For everybody's sake, she hoped it wasn't the second option.

Marcus led her directly to the cell room, rather than the lab. Even though she couldn't see anything in the darkness of the corridors, the howling getting louder was a clear indication that they were approaching the area where the rabid was held. She was going to complain about not being taken to the lab first, except that as soon as the door slid open, she realized Cyrus was there too.

Even though it was half-drugged, the rabid still reacted to her presence. Its eyes became delirious and its breathing quickened. Struggling to get up, it kept falling down and against the door, legs too weak to sustain it upright. Rage seemed to be building inside it, the bellowing getting louder and more pained. Its hand reached towards her, over and over, grasping through the air towards the impossibly far-away prey—her.

Marcus was standing quietly next to her, but she refused to look over. Instead, she stepped towards Cyrus. Each movement made the rabid more agitated, more desperate.

"I mixed the blood last night, but I was waiting for you to try it out," he said.

"What proportion?"

"One part vampire blood to thirty parts fake blood. I figured we should start with something small and see what happens," he said, producing a small vial of blood.

She looked at the glass tube in Cyrus' hands. The king's blood. "Inject him?"

"Yes, I think it would be best."

She nodded and stayed put as Cyrus and two other vampires headed towards the cell. They moved fast. So fast that it was all basically a blur of hands and flashes of color and quick bangs and snaps as they held the rabid and injected him before he had a chance to react. Just seconds after it all started, Cyrus went still next to the cage.

And a second after, the rabid slipped into a metamorphosis state. Its eyes lit up in an explosion of fire. Instead of reaching up for her in desperation, its whole body recoiled as if electricity went rushing through it. The howling that followed was so deep and so unexpected, it made her jump backwards, crashing against Marcus' chest. The rabid shook and jolted, almost as if hit by a powerful seizure, the screams rolling out louder and sharper.

Just as suddenly as it all had started, it ended. The room went deadly quiet, the body of the rabid frozen in time on the cement floor of the cell.

Her first thought was that they had killed it. Maybe Cyrus had been right all along and the poison in vampire blood had been too much for the ravaged body of the beast. She held her breath, waiting for a sign, anything, that would tell her they hadn't just made a huge mistake.

Then, a twitch. So small that she wondered if she'd imagined it. Then another. And then the rabid opened its eyes and found her. Except that instead of going insane with need, it just stayed there, watching her as she breathed heavily.

"I'll be damned," Cyrus said.

The rabid was obviously too weak to regain its vampire grandeur, but the transformation was obvious. Nothing in the outside had changed and the creature still looked like the sick beast that had been in the cage for hours. But the wailing desperation of famine was gone. In its place, there was a new calm, a savoring of the surroundings.

She took a deep breath and turned around to look at Marcus. His eyes were shining with something that looked like wonderment.

"Can we give it some more?" she asked, and the question was as much for the king as it was for Cyrus. After all, it was his blood that was feeding and healing the creature right in front of their eyes.

"Yes," Marcus said without moving his eyes away from hers.

The second shot had a similar effect. She couldn't tell if it was causing pain or if the healing process was so shocking to the system that the rabid's body twisted and warped in response to it. Either way, it was working. The convulsions lasted longer the second time around and the rabid's body hitting the ground produced deeper, heavier thuds. She had no idea how resilient its body was, but she guessed rushing the process could end up causing it serious injury. Could the violent shaking break its spine? Cause a stroke? She realized she truly knew nothing about how their bodies worked.

She was about to ask about it when the rabid went quiet. This time, it took longer to awaken, but when it did, the differences were staggering. Stumbling to its feet, the rabid shifted its weight against the bars on the door. Despite the sluggish breathing and the dazed look on its face, the beast also looked more "human" than ever before. Its movements were more calculated, somewhat fluid instead of jerky and savage as they had been just hours before.

Its eyes hovered over her for a few seconds, but this time, they didn't linger there. Instead, they zeroed on the king. She was no longer the most appealing being in the room—and that was probably the clearest sign that the blood was working.

Breathing sluggishly, the rabid leaned its head against the bars, lips moving.

Her heart pounded as the rabid whispered something too hushed for her to hear. She was trying to concentrate on the movement of the lips when she saw Cyrus' face twist in response.

She flicked her head around towards Marcus. His eyes had darkened to a bottomless black. His fangs were out and his body had turned into steel. Whatever the rabid had said, it had been loud enough for vampire ears.

A heavy weight settled on her chest. "What is it?" she whispered. "What did he say?"

Marcus' eyes remained dark and fierce as he lowered his head to look at her. "Patrick," he hissed. "He said Patrick."

CHAPTER 21

Before the letters had finished forming on the rabid's lips, he'd already guessed what they spelled. Suddenly, it all made sense: the break-ins, the rabids finding the compound, Patrick breaching the walls. Patrick would still have needed the help of somebody on the inside for all of that to happen, but the pieces were all falling into place. Marcus knew his brother well enough to see the picture clearly.

Patrick was building an army.

And his soldiers were hungry for blood and willing to kill anything and anybody that crossed their path, human or vampire.

He had always suspected Patrick wanted to build an army to one day try to overthrow him. However, he'd always thought his brother would be recruiting rogue vampires, the ones who refused to recognize Marcus' place as the king. Recruiting rabids was actually a brilliant move.

All Patrick had to do was point them in the right direction. The human scent coming from the compound would do the rest. If he sent enough rabids their way, they would have no chance. It was a simple matter of numbers. There were just over fifty vampires in the compound and maybe hundreds of rabids out there. Maybe thousands. Marcus remembered Miles' description of nearby Franklin and the vampire eyes observing them from within the darkness.

Why hadn't they attacked that night? Either Patrick was helping them find enough blood to keep them under control, or the rabids had little interest in vampires unless they smelled human blood among them.

Which meant the compound's days were numbered.

"Cyrus, get Miles," he said and only then noticed his own body in full war mode, his fangs out.

He looked down and into Belle's eyes. She didn't recoil or shrink away despite the monster showing in his face. If anything, she moved closer, a questioning look in her features.

He needed to do something and do it fast. Images of the rabids sweeping into the compound ran through his mind. He couldn't risk Belle getting caught in the wave. The minute the thought crossed his mind, he knew war was the only option.

He pulled the beast away, pushing it down until it was just a spark in the distance. By the time Miles walked into the room, he had regained enough composure to take control of the situation.

Miles' eyes zoomed in on the rabid, now in a deep sleep on the floor of the cell. Its breathing was so soft, it was hard to tell it was alive—except that Marcus could hear the beating of its heart, becoming stronger with every passing second. The blood was working, healing the beast slowly and pulling it away from madness.

"Put together the best team," he told Miles. "Twenty of the best hunters. Twenty-five. We're going back to Franklin." Miles nodded, a hint of raw determination in his eyes. Marcus knew he wouldn't need too many words to get Miles to understand what was happening. "We're going to burn the town down."

"What's Franklin?" Belle asked and her tone was not only cautious but also troubled.

He inched closer to the cage, hearing the rabid stir in his sleep. "A nearby town. I think it's where my brother is holding his army."

She gasped. "You mean he has control over the rabids? How?"

"I don't know, but it doesn't matter either. I can't risk waiting to find out." He looked back towards Miles. "We're leaving tonight."

Marcus could feel Belle's distress even before she opened her mouth. "Isn't this incredibly dangerous?" she finally said.

"Just as much as waiting here for them to attack," he answered. "Besides, Miles said they didn't attack last time they were there, right?"

"That's correct," Miles said. "They just watched us."

"So let's surprise them and burn them down. Even if we can't get all of them, burning the town down will cause them to disperse. Maybe that'll buy us some time."

"Time for what, exactly?" she asked.

"I have a feeling that many of the rabids would be on my side, not Patrick's, if it wasn't for the void." Marcus pointed towards the one in the cage. "I think that's why this one mentioned Patrick's name. He was warning us."

Her eyes grew larger. "And you want to go out there and burn them to death?"

"We don't have the luxury of time, Belle. And I can't go around catching one rabid at a time so you can inject it with blood and hope it gets cured. We're at war." He paused for a second. "You know that better than anybody."

After all, she had been the one willing to risk her life to walk into the mouth of the beast and try to kill the king.

He could see the conflict in her eyes, but this wasn't a battle he was willing to fight. Not now, when everybody's fate was holding on by the thinnest of threads. For all he knew, the attack could happen anytime. That same night, the day after. The fact that Patrick had shown up in the compound was a bad omen. Patrick had probably been testing the defenses of the place. Or maybe testing the loyalty of the traitors living in the compound.

Belle's labored breathing was pounding in Marcus' ears when he turned to Miles. "Get started. I want to leave just before it gets dark. And get the rest of the guards set up to circle the compound while we're gone."

Miles gave a quick firm nod and left. It wouldn't take long to get everything ready. Marcus hated the idea of leaving Belle behind, but this was a battle he wasn't going to miss. Because somewhere out there, probably somewhere in Franklin, his brother was waiting for him.

And he couldn't wait to once and for all kill the bastard.

~*~

A disturbing calm fell over the room once Marcus had announced his plans. As if the revelation of the upcoming attack had given everybody a new purpose. Something to look forward to.

She couldn't find the strength to get excited about it.

All she could think about was the million things that could go wrong.

He must have understood how she felt, because when he turned around to face her, his eyes were soft.

"Come with me," he said before turning towards Miles again. "Fifteen minutes."

Without waiting for an answer, he grabbed her hand and led her towards the tunnels and then out into the courtyard.

When they reached his bedroom and stepped inside, he hugged her, then reached for her mouth.

The hunger in his kiss startled her and scared her. It was as if he was kissing her for the last time. Her fingers closed over his arm, holding on to say what she couldn't put into words. *Don't go, don't do it, don't leave me here.* Slowly, he looked down and into her eyes, his hands holding her face with a determination that left her breathless.

"Marcus…"

"I'll be back, Belle," he said, his voice rolling out in a growl. "This is not goodbye."

So why does it feel like it? Her pulse was throbbing, her ears booming.

"I don't like it," she whispered and her words were tingling with uneasiness.

"I don't like it either," he admitted. "But it's time for Patrick to die."

He kissed her again, this time soft and tender. The sense of dread washing over her reached deeper, coiling and squeezing without mercy.

"I want you to stay in this room while I'm gone," he added. "It's basically a fortress. Come here."

He grabbed her hand and pulled her towards the farther end of the room. Then he pushed her palm against the wall, fingers opened and twisted in an awkward position. A soft click and the wall slid open, the darkness of the corridors oozing ahead and spilling into the room. "Nobody knows about this one except Miles and me. If anything happens, use it. It will lead you back into the tunnels."

She tried to control the shiver washing over her skin. "I hate the tunnels. It's so dark down there."

"I'm sorry, but any light will immediately alert everybody to your presence."

He let go of her and spun around, walking a few steps towards the center of the room. The door slid closed and disappeared into the wall, almost as if it never existed. The sense of doom in her chest got stronger. What if she needed to find it and couldn't? What if something came through the tunnels and broke into the room?

Stop it! her mind screamed.

Marcus turned around and reached for her. One second he was a few feet away; the next she was in his arms. And then he smiled, but the smile lacked the wickedness it usually carried. "Don't worry, you're not getting rid of me that easily."

A flash and he was on the other side of the room, opening the outside door. He hesitated for a second, then he turned around. As if he was standing at the edge of an abyss, deciding whether to jump at once or stay there for a while, savoring reality for one more impossible minute. Soft liquid silver danced in his eyes.

She took a step towards him but he raised a hand to stop her. And before he disappeared into the shadows of the courtyard, before his form blurred away into the darkness, he looked at her in a way that made her whole body ache.

"I love you, Belle," he said, and the words lingered in the air long after he was gone.

‒*‒

The next two hours were a blur of agony. She tried to run after Marcus when he stepped into the courtyard, but by the time she got to the door, he was gone. The words replayed in her head over and over as the night extended its blanket of darkness over the compound. She watched it happen from inside his bedroom, the door latched securely and the lights off. It seemed like a pointless strategy—if vampire eyes were strong enough to maneuver through the tunnels, they surely would be able to see her in the darkness of the room. But still, she let the room sit in shadows.

She placed her hand against the cold glass and felt the vibration of the night stirring against it. That was his night out there, his domain. For her, it was little more than darkness and fear.

A month ago, she would have seen the imminent danger as a potential way to get rid of the king. Now, the future of humankind depended on the king surviving the fight. Funny how things could change so quickly in a question of days. Funny how your heart could change sides before you even realized it had happened.

She had her eyes closed and her forehead against the cold glass when she heard the noise. It was just a soft rustle, fabrics brushing together. Smooth, but also foreign. A noise that didn't belong in the room.

Her eyes shot open and her pulse quickened. She looked around, trying to guess the movement of the shadows around her, but it was too dark to really tell what was hiding in the corners.

Holding her breath, she took a step towards the hidden door near the armoire—and that was when she noticed that the door separating this bedroom from hers was ajar. Ajar enough to allow for a body to pass through.

If something was in the room, it wasn't a rabid. Rabids were too desperate to be stealthy. It also wasn't a friendly vampire. Those would have come through the front door, announcing their presence.

Another step.

The rustle of fabric against air bounced on the walls, making it hard to tell where it was coming from. She was breathing so hard, it was hard to hear anything else.

Was there a guard outside her door? Probably. She could scream for help—but the vampire in the room was a lot closer to her than the one outside. She wasn't sure the guard would make it inside before she'd been torn to pieces. Any way she looked at it, the chances were not in her favor.

One more quick breath and she pressed her hand against the wall.

The second the door started to slide open, the vampire jumped out from the shadows and directly towards her. A flash of silver bursting through the air at impossible speeds. His hand brushed her arm as she plummeted into the darkness of the tunnels, but the door closed too quickly for him to make it through.

She was in complete darkness, her heart hammering madly against her chest. And then the vampire on the other side of the door let out a scream that sent waves of raw panic through her. He started pounding on the door, and she realized it wouldn't take long before he figured out how to open it.

An uproar of noises exploded in the room. Crashes of glass breaking and things being thrown around. Vampires fighting. She didn't want to wait around to see who would win.

Reaching for the nearest wall, she pressed her back against it and started sliding down the corridor. The pounding on the door made it difficult to listen to the sounds of the tunnels. She had no idea where this one went and how it connected to the underground rooms. And since she was walking blind, all she could do was to keep moving away from the door, hoping she could get far enough before the fight was over and the wrong vampire figured out the entry to the tunnels.

Because once he did, her chances of escaping were gone.

Her steps rippled in maddening echoes, bouncing above her and clinging to invisible corners. After a few feet, the corridor turned once, then again, then back around. It was impossible to keep up with it and it didn't take long before she was completely lost. The roar of the vampires in the distance was the only indication that she was still walking in the opposite direction, away from the bedroom.

It felt like she walked around for hours in the darkness, even though it couldn't have been more than a couple of minutes. Then she turned another corner and a chill rush of air hit her.

She froze, her heart pounding so wildly in her ears she couldn't hear anything else.

The tunnels had always had a suffocating feel to them, so a breeze down there could only mean one thing: the door connecting the tunnel to the outside world was open. A knot built in her throat. There was no way of knowing what was waiting for her on the other end of the tunnel. Or who was winning the battle raging back in the bedroom.

She took another step forward and then she saw it. A slight flickering in the distance, maybe fifty feet away. Black and thick and deep—but still less dark than the darkness devouring her in the tunnels.

It was the pulsing energy of the night beaming through an open door. A slight movement of air and dust against the night sky. She had to make a choice: either find her way to the open door and hope there was nothing waiting for her there. Or walk back towards the bedroom and count on the right vampire winning the fight.

Both were terrifying choices.

Like tossing a coin in the air and knowing you were lost no matter what side turned up.

Maybe if she found one of the secret rooms along the tunnel, she could hide in there until things calmed down. Except she had been walking down the tunnels for a while and hadn't come across any doors—or maybe she had but she hadn't realized it.

A bang against the sliding door on the bedroom wall made her jump. Somebody was trying to open it.

She ran her palm over the wall, somewhat hoping there would be a sliding door right there where she was standing. The walls remained silent and obscure, the whispering of the night ticking along all around her.

Another bang. Louder and this time accompanied by raging wailing. Rabids. They were inside the compound and trying to fight their way into the tunnels.

That was when she decided to run towards the night. Whatever was out there, it was probably no worse than what was waiting for her inside the compound. And at least out there she had a chance to make a run for it.

She took a deep breath, tried to focus her eyes on the promise of light in the distance and took off. It was a half-hearted run, but only because she couldn't see where she was going and the ground was too uneven to attempt a full run.

From forty feet away, the night was calling to her with open arms.

Thirty.

Twenty.

And then she tripped on something and fell forward.

She swallowed the scream rising in her throat as her hands reached forward and found a body. It was too dark to tell what it was. Probably not human, down there in the tunnels. That still left her with too many questions—the biggest one being "friend or foe?"

Because if this was a vampire who had died protecting the tunnels, it meant the enemy could be just steps ahead of her, crouched into the darkness waiting for her to walk right into it.

She got up, stepping over the body. The tunnels were so narrow in that area, she could touch both sides without completely stretching her arms.

The sound of bodies banging against metal reverberated along the tunnels. Any second now, the door would explode open and then the rabids would be on her, hungry and raging and ready for the kill. With her hands on the walls serving as guides, she tore down the rest of the tunnel, straight towards the night.

The second she stepped into the open air, the explosion of sounds assaulted her. The wind howled around the walls and into the barren landscape. She turned around to see the flames extending over the walls. Wailings of war, mixed with the sounds of humans screaming and doors being razed down, filled the night. She was alone outside the compound.

It was a ghastly sight and her first instinct was to try to run back in and find the people she knew.

Except that she wouldn't last half a minute among the rows of fangs and claws tearing at everything human inside.

So instead she took a tentative step towards one of the corners of the compound. How big was the place? Her car stood somewhere outside the walls, waiting for her. She had no idea if the keys would be in it and for all she knew the compound was miles long and she was right on the opposite side of the gate.

Her only source of light was the tongues of fire lapping over the walls. She walked towards the closest bend in the walls and took a deep breath before peeking around the corner. Empty. The walls extended at least six hundred feet into the night before they curved again in the opposite direction.

She considered crouching down or crawling along the wall, but it would take too long to reach the next corner that way. She didn't know how much time she had until the inside of the compound was gone and the vampires would step back into the night outside.

It's now or never, her mind warned her. She took off sprinting, her left arm as close to the wall as possible to help the shadows hide her.

By the time she reached the next corner, she was out of breath. Not so much from the running but from the adrenaline rushing through her. Sounds around her seemed to swell and grow, echoing into her ears and down into her chest.

Eyes closed, breath uneven, she poked her head around the corner, praying her car would be there.

When she opened her eyes, her heart skipped a beat. Her car was sitting right near the gate, just a few feet away from where she had left it before walking into the compound. Before her legs gave out or she changed her mind, she began sprinting towards it. When she found the door open and was able to jump in without trouble, a small beat of hope flashed in front of her eyes.

The roaring of the fire was deafening, leaping and reaching over and under the gate. All she was hoping for at the moment was that the sound was loud enough to hide the engine of a car.

As she switched the engine on, she glanced into the rearview mirror. The world was crumbling. In a few hours, the entire inside of the compound would be consumed by the fire. If any of the humans inside made it past the night, they'd be left to starve in the middle of nowhere, at the mercy of the four-legged predators and any rabids sick enough to venture out in daylight.

The road ahead was dark and full of uncertainty. Stepping down on the gas as far as it would go, she tried to concentrate on the actual driving. But her mind kept flying back to the compound and the horror taking place there as she ran away from it all. As she once more turned her back on humanity.

Images of Marcus returning to a destroyed compound looped around her mind as she sped down the highway.

She looked in the rearview mirror again, the compound a bright beacon of fire in the night. *Ashes to ashes, dust to dust*, her mind whispered.

"I love you too, Marcus," she said aloud.

Even if that meant damning her soul to hell.

###

Want to receive an email when my next book is released? Sign up here:

http://bit.ly/11UPJT1

Book 2 in the *Dark Tides* series is coming out later this year. Sign up at the link above to be notified when the book is released!

If you enjoyed reading this book, please consider leaving a positive review on Amazon or Goodreads. Positive reviews help increase visibility and allow me to spend more time writing and releasing books!

You can find my Goodreads page here:
http://www.goodreads.com/dibocc

ABOUT THE AUTHOR

Diana Bocco spends a lot of time thinking about vampires, warlocks and other dark creatures. Some end up in her horror books, while others have sexier destinies waiting for them.

Diana also writes nonfiction books. She currently lives in Thailand with three awesome – but slightly crazy – dogs.

Learn more about her by visiting her website at www.dianaboccobooks.com

Printed in Great Britain
by Amazon